A SUMMER AT SAGAMORE

ROMANCE IN THE GILDED AGE

LISA M. PRYSOCK

WILD HEART
BOOKS

PRAISE FOR A SUMMER AT SAGAMORE

"Light and sweet, a creampuff to satisfy the clean romance reader."

— LINORE ROSE BURKARD, AWARD-WINNING AUTHOR

"Who can resist a typewriter-toting heroine and a dashing hero with the last name of Gable? With hints of Jane Austen combined with romance and mystery in the Gilded Age, Lisa M. Prysock's *A Summer at Sagamore* is a sparkling gem sure to satisfy every reader's heart!"

— JOANN DURGIN, USA TODAY BESTSELLING AUTHOR OF *THE LEWIS LEGACY SERIES*

For my lovely daughter, Courtney

CHAPTER 1

It was June, and the world smelled of roses. The sunshine was like powdered gold over the grassy hillside.

— MAUD HART LOVELACE

JUNE OF 1907

*A*t the beginning of every summer, Abby thought the world lay at her feet. Anything could happen in the span of three months—seldom lasting long enough—but always months filled with bliss, wonder, and escape. From aboard the Sagamore steamboat, Abigail Rose Greenwood reveled in the views of natural beauty surrounding them in the wilds of what comprised only a mere glimpse of the millions of acres known as the Adirondack Park. She found herself speechless at the unfolding glory, unlike her travel companions as they stood alongside the upper deck's rails. The ship plowed steadily forward, cutting a path through blue-green waves and pristine waters splashing below them, the gale making her feel alive with anticipation as they neared their destination.

"I can't wait to see the Sagamore Resort." Abby's younger sister Catherine stretched out her arms over the railing to embrace the wind blowing her brunette curls around her shoulders, her brown eyes wide and bright. Seventeen, she glowed with apparent excitement about the adventure.

"Patience, my dear. We will arrive at Green Island in a few minutes. Enjoy the fresh air and the boat ride, girls." Her face alight, wisps of Grandmother's silver and white hair wafted in the breeze around her face. She had coifed her silvery hair into a smooth knot beneath the stylish hat pinned firmly to her head, leaving Abby wondering how many pins kept her hat from blowing away into the wind and waves. Except for her cane and silvery hair, who would take Fanny Wiltshire for a wealthy widow in her seventies? She hardly had any wrinkles or creases in her smooth complexion. Abby and Catherine had inherited her brown eyes, and dark hair from their father, but their cousin had inherited Grandmother's once golden-brown hair.

"It was kind of your friend to recommend such a popular refuge for this year's summer excursion, Gran." Cousin Elizabeth, two years younger than Abby at nineteen, looked pretty as a picture holding onto her hat beneath its layers of tulle, her golden-brown wavy hair streaming away from her face in the wind, blue eyes shining. "And I cannot wait to see the Sagamore either." A mischievous grin appeared on her face which she only shared with her cousins when Grandmother turned her attention toward the tree line along the banks of Lake George.

"Yes, it was." Gran nodded absentmindedly, focused on the view.

Abby knew her cousin's grin had more to do with finding a handsome beau from among the gentlemen who would surely also be found spending the summer months in the rugged luxury awaiting them at the fashionable resort.

While Elizabeth turned away from the railing and scanned the other passengers aboard the steamboat— Abby guessed to catch the eye of a well-dressed gentleman or admirer—she turned her thoughts to the previous leg of their journey. Early that morning, they'd embarked on a train from New York City to upstate New York. The scenery had captured Abby's attention from the start as tall buildings disappeared from the horizon, yielding to countryside thick with lush meadows, picturesque farms, and tree-covered mountains. Once they'd transferred to the steamboat, the farther they traveled, the more the mountain and lake views stunned her into silence, stealing her breath away, filling her with the wonder and awe of

God's creation. On top of these magnificent delights, the small passenger vessel carried them past glorious mansion after mansion, a long line of impressive summer homes along the western side of Lake George.

"Girls, you are now viewing what has been dubbed *Millionaire's Row* on Lake George," Grandmother informed them as they feasted on the sights.

The grand line of mansions situated against the magnificent splendor of nature seemed intoxicating enough, but then Green Island came into view and the steamship glided to a stop, anchoring at a dock called Bolton's Landing.

"We are here at last," Catherine breathed as she caught sight of something and standing up taller, craned to see something on their right. "I cannot wait to attend the dances, swim in the glorious new bathing pool, and try out the tennis court."

Abby squinted to see what held her sister's attention. Ah! Of course. A group of teen boys about her age gathered on the docks, preparing to row some small boats somewhere, perhaps fishing for the day.

"Don't forget picnics and horseback riding." Elizabeth elbowed Abby and nodded toward a trio of finely dressed gentlemen looking toward the ship from the landing, awaiting someone's arrival maybe. When a crew member on a lower deck tossed them a bundle of newspapers and one of them caught it, Abby realized why they waited.

"My, aren't they handsome?" Elizabeth whispered, opening her parasol since the ship had anchored.

"Indeed." She smiled, turning her attention to steal her first glimpse at the Sagamore Resort. Nestled in the trees, the impressive resort had evaded them until now. It didn't disappoint, standing atop the island like a proud king, welcoming its visitors. She could hardly wait to take in the view from land.

Among a steady stream of disembarking passengers, Abby and her family became separated. Lugging her typewriter case in one hand, she stepped onto the island ahead of them with a mixture of relief, apprehension, and hope. Not even the heaviness of her typewriter could diminish the experience. Breathing in the fresh air, she inhaled the smell of tall pines and wild bergamot mingled with the scent of nasturtium, roses, foxglove, and asters in the well-tended flowerbeds. Yes, this was definitely an improvement over New York City —and even over their home city, Cincinnati. As much as she'd enjoyed having Grandmother indulge and spoil them with purchases of the latest fashions and accoutrements needed to greet summer with confidence, she'd thrive in the wilderness—well, from the security of the comforts of Sagamore. Although Green Island didn't hold quite the same appeal as many of their previous destinations in Europe, it offered an attraction of another kind. This island playground tucked in a rustic, hidden paradise warmly extended safe harbor and inspiration.

Cousin Elizabeth caught up to Abby. "This certainly is a better view than the industrial side of downtown Los Angeles last summer, though I will cherish the friends we made and all we learned on Azusa Street. What a difference the Sagamore will be from the mission." She sighed while tugging a glove more securely over her wrist.

"Indeed. Azusa transformed us all like a Red Sea, defining moment. I think Sagamore will carry us into our promised-land destiny," Abby remarked while men from the steamship's sparse crew hoisted trunks, loading them onto a horse-drawn cart. She wished she could trust one of them with her typewriter, but she did not dare. "This reminds me of Portugal, of our seaside lodgings on the cliffs, except these waters are far more pristine, and we're more secluded."

Elizabeth placed her hands on her hips. "I guess it does remind me of Portugal."

Catherine caught up to them next, breathless with anticipation, Gran a few steps behind. "Just look at the bathing pool! We are in heaven. I do wonder which balcony and windows are ours. Did you request a villa or a suite facing Lake George, Grandmama?" Her big brown eyes and vivacious smile reflected her excitement as she twirled her open parasol around against her shoulder.

Grandmother paused beside them and peered up at the main house, leaning heavily on her cane. "Of course, I did. Not a villa, but a balcony suite in the main house so we don't have to hike back and forth to the dining rooms. You don't think me a reckless fool, do you?" Grandmother glanced at her youngest grand-daughter, Catherine, and then at Abby. "Abigail would find the manager and bargain away our valuables until we had the very best view available."

Abby laughed, remembering a few occasions when Gran had called upon her to use her kind manners of persuasion. "I am ready upon your command to argue with the front desk clerk if anything is found unsuitable or lacking. I can't imagine that here, however."

"You are my only grandchild who can argue in French or Italian equally well," Gran marveled.

Elizabeth stepped forward, leading the way on the path up the hill, holding onto her hat as she gazed at the resort. "Let's not dawdle lest they give our suite away to someone else. Shall we, ladies?"

"We shall." Abby nodded and resumed lugging her typewriter case uphill, following behind her cousin. "I think we will be very happy here, Grandmother."

"I do hope so, girls," Gran stepped in beside Eliza-beth. "It's not my grand estate in Marietta overlooking the Ohio River, but the view is marvelous. Catherine, you'll room with your sister since you are accustomed to the writing contraption, and Elizabeth, you shall room with me. We'll share a private sitting room between the bedrooms, and the suite has our own powder room with a bathing tub. I'm famished, ready for tea, unpacking, and then a lie-down as soon as we are properly settled. I will ask the clerk to send tea for four to our suite."

"Yes, Grandmother. The arrangements will be splendid. I'm delighted to share a room with my sister again." Catherine stuck her tongue out at Abby as they trudged along behind Elizabeth and Gran.

Abby rolled her eyes at her younger sister's customary antics. Did she detect a slight sigh escape Elizabeth? No one liked to sleep with Grandmother. She sometimes snored like a locomotive, talked in her sleep, and required assistance with all sorts of errands and tasks.

"Let's go inside, and for heaven's sake, don't stick your tongue out anymore. It's vulgar," Abby whispered. Nearing the entrance, she couldn't help but notice an attractive, fashionably dressed gentleman standing off to one side of the front porch, observing the arriving guests, surrounded by a flock of ladies gushing over him. He had stared at them as they'd trudged uphill while she'd lugged the heavy typewriter. A true gentleman would have excused himself from his admirers and offered to assist her, but he hadn't stepped away from the three ladies buzzing about him.

Catherine shrugged. "But it annoys you, and I must keep up with my reputation."

"Shall we call a truce for the summer?" Abby proposed, unable to avoid the view of the man's figure in his white summer suit. Tall and dashing, with dark hair parted to one side, he studied them with amusement in his blue eyes as he leaned against a pillar on the front porch. One of the ladies in the flock rearranged his tie while another tucked her arm around his elbow. He had attractive crow's feet in the corners of his eyes, a broad chest span, and a well-developed, muscular build. He might be twenty-seven or twenty-eight. She guessed she could understand why he drew the ladies to his side, but couldn't he see she could use a little help? The bellhops, busy assisting other passengers, hadn't seen them approaching the front doors yet, but the man staring at them certainly had.

"Truce," Catherine agreed, reluctance in her voice, snapping Abby's attention back to how she would get the heavy typewriter across the porch and inside to their suite.

The fellow had likely overheard their conversation since he'd hardly taken his eyes off them as they'd progressed onto the porch. Looking away as heat warmed her cheeks, she hoped he wouldn't see her blush.

Did he like her brown eyes? But didn't almost every heroine in novels have blue eyes? She aimed to write her heroines with brown eyes. In any case, Abby chided herself. What did she know of him to care, other than his handsome looks? He seemed arrogant and intrusive, the way he grinned at her as if he knew all her secrets. Couldn't the gentleman pause from tending the flock of socialites to open the door for them?

Why did he stand there gawking at arriving guests,

anyway? She averted her eyes, patting her brunette updo to make sure all remained in place as a bellhop appeared and held the door open. They entered the main foyer, allowing her to sweep past the handsome stranger before she collapsed from the weight of her typewriter. She figured it weighed nearly a fifth of her body weight. She could hardly wait to find their suite and forget the rake.

---

*O*nce they'd taken the elevator, explored their lodgings, reveled in the view, and more bellhops delivered their trunks, Gran busied herself with unpacking in her bedroom while waiting on their tea. The girls ended up in the room Catherine would share with Abby, Elizabeth filing in last. Closing the door, their cousin fell against it and sighed with a dreamy look on her face.

Catherine flung herself across one of the double beds and then Elizabeth fell across the other while Abby used her foot to push her typewriter case toward the desk beneath the window. Since she would need a rest before lifting it onto the desk, she perched on the end of the bed and released a long sigh. They had arrived at last.

"Did you see how many handsome gentlemen are swarming the foyer, the front lawn, and the drawing room?" Elizabeth clasped her hands to her heart, glee in her voice. "Everywhere I look, there are more."

Catherine rolled over onto her stomach and released a groan. "How shall we ever narrow our choices down to only one?"

Abby chuckled, catching the pillow Catherine tossed in her direction. She collapsed on it from her perch and now lay on her side, facing her sister and cousin. Mission accomplished, having lugged her precious typing machine this far, she could now relax and unpack. Her boy-crazy companions however, had other matters in mind.

Elizabeth rolled over to her side, facing Abby and Catherine. A sobering look came over her face, but then a coy smile appeared as she entwined a curl, wrapping it around and around one of her fingers. "You know the rules. One week. We each have one week to decide on whom we shall place our deepest affection and unswerving devotion for the summer, apart from the Lord, that is. He must remain first in our hearts, of course. I do hope to find a fellow worthy of my affection. Maybe someone of means and wealth, I hope."

Bravo, Elizabeth—except for the part about finding a man of means and wealth. Money didn't amount to everything. Elizabeth would always be Abby's cantankerous cousin, but their experience at Azusa appeared to have wrought some change to the storekeeper's daughter who only a year ago had struggled with holding onto faith, let alone a mention of the Lord.

"I know the other rule, only if we reserve the right at the time of choosing may we change our mind and choose a different beau to adore if we have misgivings, unless some other beau we like chooses one among us." Catherine rolled over onto her back and stared at the ceiling, her hands folding over her abdomen. "So many choices and so little time. I must have counted at least a dozen boys of my age and we've only been here five minutes."

"I would begin by eliminating the boys who are too short. That will leave you with less to concern yourself about. You can focus on their inner qualities such as kindness and integrity, and well ... other things." Elizabeth mused, causing the three of them to burst into laughter. Gran would soon hear them carrying on and knock on the door, insisting one of them pour tea, another fetch her slippers, and one bring her favorite wrap to her side. Then she would persuade them to tell her of their summer plans and fall into a pleasant rest immediately after.

Abby couldn't deny the fact her heart blossomed with the hope something wonderful could happen in the months ahead. She'd set her mind on finishing her manuscript, embracing the carefree lifestyle of summertime, and exploring Green Island. Nothing but the pursuit of these three things entered her mind, though Catherine and Elizabeth longed for romance. No, indeed. Abby would spend her life as a writer. Since her ideal husband only existed in romantic novels, she'd long ago decided against the institution of marriage. What if she ended up married to someone who didn't treat her with kindness or worse, someone who clipped her wings? Perhaps an attractive rake who wouldn't lift a finger to open doors or help her with a heavy typewriter, for instance.

CHAPTER 2

The earth had donned her mantle of brightest green; and shed her richest perfumes abroad. It was the prime and vigor of the year; all things were glad and flourishing.

— CHARLES DICKENS, *OLIVER TWIST*

"To be clear, I'm only agreeing to one twenty-minute horseback ride. I plan to spend the rest of the day writing, enjoying the splendid view of Lake George from our suite. Gran did well in securing such magnificent rooms for us." Abby sipped the last of her coffee and took another bite of her scrambled eggs the next morning in the resort's spacious dining room. Floor-to-ceiling floral curtains fluttered in the breeze from the open windows.

"Fair enough, and I can't agree more. Granny did

well." Cousin Elizabeth reached for more honey and began drizzling some on her oatmeal.

"Of course, I did. We shan't return if they give us a view we can't appreciate." Grandmother tasted some of her soft-boiled egg served in an elegant egg cup.

"How are your Eggs and Soldiers, Gran?" Abby inquired as her grandmother dipped a stick of toast in the egg.

"Almost as delicious as when eating it in London," Grandmother replied.

"You'll die for lack of sunshine if you don't spend more time outdoors, Abby. Twenty minutes hardly seems long enough." Catherine sliced into her fried egg, observing her. "The ride will do us all good. We surely don't do enough riding living in a brownstone in Cincinnati where everything is a short walk away and you spend most of your time hiding in the garret writing your stories."

Did Abby detect concern from Katie-bug? Her left brow rose as she considered this new personality seated in the cane-back chair beside her. "I do believe you're worried about my health. Are you sure you aren't coming down with a temperature?"

"Maybe I'm more mature than you credit me for, Abs." Catherine flipped her brown locks over one shoulder. "Would you please pass the teapot?"

"I'll reserve judgement on the subject of your maturity until the next time you stick your tongue out." Abby slid the teapot in her sister's direction and reached for more of the blackberry jam for the buttermilk biscuit on her plate, catching a glimpse of the handsome rake she'd seen at the main entrance as he entered the breakfast room. The maître d' led him to a table with a few other gentlemen his age. A waitress took his order and poured him a cup of coffee while Grandmother shared her plan to take a leisurely walk on the grounds and then read a book on their suite's balcony.

"You aren't going walking alone, are you, Grandmother?" Catherine asked.

Grandmother shook her head. "No. I plan to read, sip tea, and take a walk with Mrs. VanDyne from our neighboring suite, and get into whatever trouble I may find while my granddaughters are otherwise engaged."

"Sounds nice, Grandmother." Abby tasted the biscuit. Why did the blackberry jam taste better here than elsewhere? She could indulge in many more biscuits smothered with it if she let herself.

Gran reached for her goblet of orange juice. "Don't forget to dress in time for dinner at seven. It's served in the main dining room."

As conversation swirled around her, Abby became lost in her thoughts about the next chapter in her manuscript and the fact Mr. Handsome had attracted another flock of socialites around his table. She pretended not to notice, keeping her eyes on the windows instead. When her sister and cousin rose at the conclusion of the meal, she did likewise, making a concerted effort not to glance in the handsome stranger's direction. Her back burned. Was he watching?

Gran looked up at her granddaughters. "Go and have a wonderful time, girls. I'm going to linger over the newspaper with more tea. Do be careful. Your mothers will never forgive me if any of you are injured. And remember, if you go to the pool, boys on one side, girls on the other."

"We will be careful," Elizabeth promised. "But after our ride, Catherine and I are playing badminton and headed to the pool later. We also signed up for ballroom dancing lessons. There are all sorts of activities to sign up for in the foyer. You might enjoy the book club, Grandmama."

"The book club does sound appealing." Grandmother smiled. "If you ask me, badminton is far more enjoyable than tennis. I never could keep up on the tennis court. I don't think it's in our blood."

Abby chuckled as they each gave their grandmother a kiss on the cheek. "I secretly agree. No tennis for me. I'm more interested in the swimming pool and time to write. See you after our ride, Gran." With her head high, she led the way to the foyer—the long way around, to avoid the rake's table ... and his searing gaze.

*B*y the end of the first week, she'd managed to avoid Mr. Handsome by keeping a rigorous writing schedule—apart from seeing him at meals. On Friday at noon, the girls convinced Abby to spend the rest of the day with them at the pool where Gran had already situated herself with Mrs. VanDyne and some of the book club ladies.

Abby added the last page of a completed chapter to the stack of papers on her desk, smiling at her first week of writing progress. "All right. Give me ten minutes to change." She picked up her manuscript and tucked it in a drawer, away from prying eyes.

She ducked behind the dressing screen and hurried into swimming pantalets, matching tunic, belt, hat, and finally, the swimming slippers. They'd purchased their bathing suits in New York City from Bloomingdale's, and no one could say they looked anything but charming and fashionable.

While donning the navy-and-white nautical attire, she hummed "Melody of Love," a popular tune released in 1903. She remembered the year because she'd had a secret beau who'd inspired her to sing the song during the short-lived fling when she had turned seventeen ... Hank Hartman, one of the only boys to ever turn her head. Would she find Mr. Handsome at the pool? She couldn't help but wonder.

After a refreshing swim on the girls' side of the pool, they climbed out to recline in lounge chairs. Servers brought them beverages, plates of potato salad, deviled eggs, and orange segments, ensuring guests had everything they could want. Sure enough, she spotted Mr. Handsome on the other side of the pool with some other gentlemen about his age.

"All right, ladies, it's been a week," Elizabeth said in a low voice. "You know what that means."

Katie-bug giggled and lowered her voice too. "Time for our annual summer adoration picks."

"No, I can't." Abby rolled her eyes. "I just can't. There are too many here, and I haven't spent enough time away from my typewriter to ponder this."

"Of course, you can. It's tradition." Her sister playfully jabbed her elbow.

"You see the best of those present on the opposite corner of the pool deck. Surely, one of these gentlemen have caught a glimpse of your attention," Elizabeth tossed her a mischievous grin. "It's harmless fun, after all. Besides, one of these days, you'll soon be urged to marry someone. Grandmother might say you can't inherit if you don't marry."

Which of Catherine's and Elizabeth's points demanded a response? Maybe the knowledge of her future inheritance played a hand in her desire to remain independent, but she'd learned the art of discretion. If she voiced her plan not to marry, forces might conspire against her. Besides, what if she changed her mind? Better to remain silent and free about serious decisions and matters of the heart. Grandmother had never hinted at forcing her into a marriage in order to retain her inheritance. Gran had set aside funds for Catherine and Elizabeth, too, and she had never indicated conditions.

"I suppose you have a point insomuch as seldom does anything ever come of it," Abby conceded. "One of us might have our attention returned by an admirer with a dance or two."

"If we are exceptionally lucky, a kiss." Elizabeth puckered her lips and made them giggle. "Not that any of us believe in luck."

Abby smiled, relieved she wouldn't have to convince Elizabeth yet again that she and Catherine had not been raised to believe in luck as minister's daughters. Perhaps last year's trip to Los Angeles and the Azusa Street Mission had stuck with her cousin more than Elizabeth let on. Reverend Greenwood, Abigail and Catherine's father, had taught them to look for and appreciate the many ways the Lord watched over them, even in the smallest of life's details. He often made a game of counting their blessings to reinforce this point. Abby and Catherine had played it with Elizabeth a number of times over the summers they'd shared.

Elizabeth fiddled with the large buttons on her swimming outfit, her elbows on the arms of her lounge chair. "I choose that very handsome gentleman with the light-brown hair named Ryan. He shall be the fellow I admire from afar this summer, but it is my hope he will become my true love. His name is all I know about him, other than I don't believe he is staying at the resort. He's either a local from the town of Bolton, or perhaps a son of one of these millionaires who live on the Lake George row."

"Why do you say that?" Abby sat forward, studying the said gentleman, who wore the latest fashion in men's swimming attire as he tossed a tennis ball to one of the other fellows in his company.

"He often arrives in time for breakfast or returns at dinner on a rowing boat every few days to spend time with the others, and I also saw him arrive on a steam yacht one day. I'm guessing he grew up around here and some of these gentlemen summer together each year. He seems to know them well. Anyhow, you can see how strong and tan he is from rowing his boat. He also dresses exceptionally nice and is so very tall and handsome. Your turn, Katie."

"My summer adoration is easy this year." Catherine's eyes traveled to a different corner where some of the younger boys gathered. "His name is Edwin. He has wavy brown hair I would love to run my hands through." She paused while they laughed. "He played badminton with us this week, and I overheard him tell someone he's seventeen, so I know we are the same age. I've also figured out he has a brother and two sisters. I suspect they are here on a family vacation, but I don't know for how long. His sisters are in our dance class. He's often waiting to do something with them after the lesson. Your turn, Abs."

"All right." Abby sighed, reluctance evident in her voice. "I'll play along, although I've outgrown the game." In truth, her attraction this year seemed stronger than in previous summers, though she'd hardly tell them that. "He's the fellow seated in the lounge chair beside Elizabeth's Ryan. I know absolutely nothing about him except I think he's handsome, confident, and dresses nicely. Sometimes I think he's an utter rake, and other times, I'm not so sure."

"What makes you think he's a rake?" Elizabeth asked, leaning closer, appearing eager to hear her response.

"I don't know," Abby attempted to sound nonchalant. "The way he attracts socialites and seems to thrive on their attention, for one thing. The way he looks at me, for another. He could have held the door for us when we arrived and offered to help carry my typewriter when the bellhops were busy. Other times, I see him taking a walk on the lawn or after dinner reading the newspapers in the drawing room with the other gentlemen, mainly keeping to himself. One evening, I saw him help an elderly guest down the steps of the front porch, and I thought I'd misjudged him too early. Maybe he's been here before and all of the regular socialites just happen to know him." She could tell her audience understood what she meant. "My overactive writer imagination cannot decide between the contrasting sides of him from what little I know."

"We do know you wouldn't trust anyone to help

with your typewriter, Abs," Catherine pointed out, causing them to laugh again.

"You're absolutely right." Abby laughed with them at herself.

"Your typewriter is heavy. I can see why you'd be disappointed he didn't offer to hold the door open," Elizabeth said in a low voice.

"Exactly." Abby nodded.

"And he can't help drawing the attention of the ladies. He's too old for me, but I'll admit he is attractive, which is a bonus for you," Catherine acknowledged, making them smile about his good looks.

For a moment, they held their silence. It gave Abby a moment to relish the outdoors and study the bathing pool against the backdrop of Lake George, shimmering in the sunshine.

"There are all sorts of events coming up with chances to encounter our summer loves ..." Catherine's voice held a wistful tone. "Picnics, tennis tournaments, golf and hiking outings, and even yacht parties."

"Take heed, little sister. It's nice to dream, but don't get your hopes too high and end up with a broken heart," Abby warned. "Keep an open mind to other fellows at Sagamore. I reserve the right to choose someone else. There are plenty of handsome fish to catch on this lake, from what I can see from this chair."

"I'll say," Elizabeth agreed as she stared at a handsome young man passing by the edge of the pool on his way to join the gentlemen and teen boys on the other side. A grin spread across her lips as she averted her eyes from the gentleman, but the three of them couldn't help but laugh again.

When Abby looked up, her eyes met the gaze of Mr. Handsome at hearing their laughter. She wondered if this year might bring more than laughter, even as she considered the downsides to her attractive rake.

CHAPTER 3

All in all, it was a never to be forgotten summer—
one of those summers which come seldom into any
life, but leave a rich heritage of beautiful memories
in their going—one of those summers which, in a
fortunate combination of delightful weather,
delightful friends, and delightful doing, come as
near to perfection as anything can come in this
world.

— LUCY MAUDE MONTGOMERY,
ANNE'S HOUSE OF DREAMS

"*D*o tell us what your book is about, Abigail,"
Cousin Elizabeth prodded as they brought
their horses to a rest at the crest of a small
hill atop a meadow they'd ridden through at a gallop.

"No." Abby chuckled while giving her cousin a look of exasperation as she patted her horse. Three times, they'd asked about her book in the past week, and three times, she'd escaped giving them the satisfaction of any details. Didn't they know writers thrived on privacy?

"Why ever not?" Catherine sounded indignant.

Abby sighed as her horse did a sideways step to avoid a pesky mosquito. "Because, number one, I'm not finished. Number two, it may never be published. Number three, it's hard enough coping with the idea it may be rejected by publishers. Number four, the subject matter is controversial. There, I've given you more than enough information. I require secrecy to see it through, or I shall despair and give up."

"I see," Catherine replied, her tone softer. "It's hard to understand writers. Sometimes you tell me what you're writing, and other times, it's a secret."

Abby could feel her sister studying her from astride her mount, but she kept her gaze straight ahead on the cluster of ladies and gentlemen riding horses about fifty yards away from them, her handsome stranger among the riders. She'd seen him riding on a few other occasions, often in Ryan's company and with others of about the same age. She still didn't know her handsome stranger's name, but he always looked attractive with his dark hair parted on one side, his blue eyes resilient with the hint of a twinkle. He looked especially attractive today wearing a loose-fitting white shirt, beige riding breeches which did little to hide his muscular build, and fashionable black riding boots.

When the group of seven riders turned toward the stable, Elizabeth waited until they passed around the far side of the meadow from the crest where the three of them rested astride their horses. Then she pulled on the leather reins and steered her horse in the same direction. "Let's catch up with the others. I'm ready for our badminton tournament, and I see my Ryan in the group. I'm hoping to casually bump into him when we arrive at the stable."

Abby liked the idea of returning so she could get on with her writing. Maybe she, too, would brush shoulders with her stranger. Would he stay at the Sagamore for the duration of the summer, or would he depart before she could meet him? Why did he travel without family? Had she imagined him staring at her last night at dinner? Questions darted through her mind as she and Katie-bug steered their horses to follow Elizabeth's mare. Leaning forward in their saddles, they urged the horses into a sprint through the meadow, the other riders now only a short distance ahead and to the right.

As the pack of riders passed under a patch of trees spreading their leaves in various shades of green overhead, Abby squinted in the morning sunshine. Had they room to pass under the limbs? When all seven riders emerged from the trees without having to sit low or lean forward too much, she relaxed her hold on the reins, free from worry until they reached the creek.

If she let her mare maintain a decent speed and remembered to rise in her saddle a bit and lean into the jump, she and Mallory could sail over the narrow stream without trouble. She could tell Mallory liked to jump since she'd landed every obstacle they'd attempted with clean strides and on solid footing.

The first five riders breezed through the jump over the creek, but the next—a lady Abby recognized as Miss Lena Carter after meeting her while reading books on the resort's porch one afternoon—screamed when her saddle slipped to the right as her horse landed on the other side. Lena couldn't hang on, falling in a heap about five feet past the creek. Lena's horse hadn't been able to slow, and it was all Abby, Elizabeth, and Catherine could do to navigate around the horse and the downed rider, since like the others, they'd flown over the creek at a decent speed to cross safely.

Once Abby's horse landed the jump, she steered the mare to one side and pulled the reins, bringing Mallory to a stop. The handsome stranger, Elizabeth, Catherine, and three other riders did the same, turning back to tend Miss Carter.

Abby dismounted, reaching Lena first, and knelt to see how she could help, though as the lady was an experienced rider from a Kentucky horse farm, she might not wish for assistance. "Miss Carter, Lena ... are you all right?" Was she conscious? Abby gently shook Lena's arm until her eyes fluttered open. "Is anything broken, Miss Carter? Thank goodness, you've landed in some shrubbery. I think it broke your fall."

"I-uh-I don't think anything is bro-broken, but I'm scratched up from those prickly things ... and my elbow ... th-throbs." Lena winced, her eyes closing again as she touched her head. "I think I'm going to have a lump the size of Mount Everest. I'm okay but sh-shaken."

"Do you think you can sit up? Would you like to ride back on my horse?" Abby asked, vaguely aware the handsome stranger had decided to pursue Lena's horse.

"Yes, I think I can sit up. That would be very nice of you, Miss Greenwood, to lend me your horse after I've lost mine." Lena blinked rapidly as Elizabeth and Catherine dismounted.

"Are you all right?" Elizabeth knelt beside Abby and Lena while Catherine hovered. Ryan stood nearby, listening to the exchange, his gaze darting around, looking for something. Perhaps he wondered about the saddle as Abby did.

Abby caught the others up. "Miss Carter seems to be intact other than some scratches from the shrubs and a bump on her head and elbow. No broken bones as far as she can tell, but perhaps a trip to the infirmary is in order." She turned back to the injured rider. "Just rest a few moments, and then we'll help you onto my horse when you're ready."

"V-very good," Lena stammered. "I'm more shocked than anything else. A few lumps, bumps, and bruises. It could have been much worse. I'm thankful for the prickly shrubs."

The handsome stranger returned to them, leading Lena's horse by the reins.

"Thanks, Jack. Good thinking to recover her horse. I wonder where the saddle landed," the one named Ryan said. "Is that it over there?"

Abby looked up at her handsome stranger. Jack. His name was Jack. Ryan found the faulty saddle a few feet beyond the shrubs and hoisted it onto Lena's mount, securing it with rope. Odd, that he didn't inspect it. Why had it slipped off in the first place?

"Let me have a look at the saddle." Jack stepped closer to Lena's horse and began inspecting the remains of the belt hanging beneath the girth of the horse. *Good man! Bravo!* Something caught his eye in the shrubs. He picked up another piece to the strap containing the buckle. He reexamined the part of the strap attached to the saddle, then the broken piece again. "Here's the problem. The strap still attached to the saddle looks as if it's been cut to this point right here on the back side of the leather. See where it ripped the rest of the way into a more jagged tear?" Jack showed Ryan the strap. "I'm afraid to say, it looks intentional, but I can't say so for sure, or how long it's been in this condition. My guess is, not long enough for experienced stable hands to notice since it's on the reverse side and wasn't cut all the way through."

"Disturbing," Abby commented, her voice fading.

Everyone else wore a pensive look. "Miss Carter is an expert rider. The Carters own a horse farm in Lexington, Kentucky. No wonder she was able to hang on for as long as she did. Good riding experience."

"Thank you for pointing that out." Lena gingerly finger-searched the back of her head. "I was fine until the saddle began slipping."

Ryan patted Jack on the back. "Good work, Jack, finding the other piece to the saddle strap."

Jack nodded and put the severed piece to the strap in his pocket. "I'll show this to the stable manager. Miss Carter handled it better than most would have. I'm going to have a look around and see if I can find anything else."

A short while later, the ladies and Ryan helped Miss Carter to her feet and onto Abby's horse. Abby introduced her sister and cousin to Lena once she had mounted. Elizabeth and Catherine agreed to escort her the rest of the way to the stable, their horses moving along on either side of Mallory as escorts. Ryan mounted and began riding toward the stable with the reins to Lena's horse in his hands.

Leading his stallion, Jack approached Abby as the others trotted away. "Care to ride with me, uh, Miss ...?"

"Miss Abigail Greenwood," Abby supplied. Hm, interesting development. A chance to ride with her handsome mystery man.

"Jackson Gable." He held out his hand to shake hers. "Let's get you into the saddle. It's too far to walk."

"It's very kind of you to share your horse." Abby eyed his massive stallion.

"You gave yours to Miss Carter. Here, I'll give you a hand up." Before Abby could protest, he'd picked her up and placed her on the horse sidesaddle. Then he swung up into the seat behind her, and his strong arms enveloped her as he grasped the reins. "Hold on tight."

Abby held onto the front of the saddle as they progressed, then gave in to also clasping one of his arms to keep her balance, but his strong arms around her gave her an assurance she hadn't felt for some time. Her heartbeat sped from such close proximity to Mr. Handsome. Clinging to his forearm seemed forward, but she had no choice unless she wanted to land on the ground in similar fashion to Miss Carter.

"So, Miss Greenwood," Jack said as he steered them toward the stables, "tell me about yourself. Where are you from?"

"I'm from Cincinnati, and you?" She breathed in, so close to him, she couldn't help but notice Jack smelled of sandalwood, pine trees, and saddle leather.

"Philadelphia," he replied.

"And what do you do whilst in Philadelphia?" A glance over her shoulder revealed she had earned a smile.

"Until recently, I've been away at a university and haven't been home except for brief visits."

"I see. Do you have family living there? In Philadelphia?"

"I do," he said. "One sister, one maternal aunt, and my parents. And you, do you have family in Cincinnati, Miss Greenwood?"

"I do. My parents." Not as annoyed with him as she had found herself when she'd first met him, she decided she would permit him to be less formal. She liked the way he had behaved in this situation they found themselves in through no fault of their own. "And please, call me Abby. My sister is here, along with our cousin and my grandmother."

"Ah, so you are too well-chaperoned for me to ride off into the distance with you to never be seen again?" he quipped, sounding flirtatious.

Abby laughed at his clichéd yet poetic remarks, one of her brows rising. "Indeed. Are you at Sagamore for the summer, or a brief visit?"

"Since I've met you, I'll probably stay around much longer." He wore another of his amused looks and when she twisted to look at him, she could see he studied her for a reaction.

"Now you are teasing me when I am only trying to keep polite conversation." She decided he was enjoying this a little too much, but then, so did she, finding him more charming than she had expected.

"I digress. I set out for Sagamore intending to stay until I weary of it," he confessed.

"And your friend Ryan?" Curious, she had to ask, for Elizabeth's sake.

"He's a local, so I assume he, too, will be around a while."

"I see. Well, here we are. Thank you for the ride." Abby allowed him to dismount and then he helped her down, his strong hands manly around her waist. Their adventure might be coming to an end, but at least she and Elizabeth had chosen gentlemen to adore who would not depart anytime soon.

CHAPTER 4

Before I formed thee in the belly I knew thee; and before thou camest forth out of the womb I sanctified thee, and I ordained thee a prophet unto the nations.

— JEREMIAH 1:5

*A*bby's ride to the stables, though short lived, had given her the beginning bonds of acquaintance with Jackson Gable. She had remained silent while he and Ryan relayed the information about her friend's accident to August, the stable manager, as his two assistants, Stan and Fred, looked on and examined the saddle. Before seeking remedy for Lena's injuries at the resort, Lena, Elizabeth, and Catherine had shared their versions of the story as well. August and his helpers found the condition of the saddle alarming too. They vowed to do their best to discover what could have happened.

From then on, Abby could accept and return Jack's nods in her direction and even strike up a conversation with him in casual passing on Sagamore's grounds if she wanted. He flirted like a rake, and she had to determine if he only did so with her, or every woman who piqued his curiosity. After all, she had her writing to tend. And if she had any hope of nourishing her slight romantic interest in Jack, she couldn't let him know she had any attraction to him whatsoever.

After a day or two, the resort buzzed with the news of Miss Lena Carter's horseback riding accident. Knowledge of the incident spread like wildfire through the guests, but the stable still thrived with activity as undaunted patrons continued to ride, except for Lena. That lady gave herself a week of rest and spent much of her time reading a book in a lounge chair on the front porch or from the privacy of her suite's balcony. How lonely she looked. One day after tea with Grandmother, Abby took a book and joined Lena on the porch overlooking the island's front, east-facing lawn.

"I see you are recovering nicely. I'm sure your parents are thankful," Abby said after settling into the chaise beside her friend.

Lena smiled. "Thank you, and yes, Father thinks the saddle was deliberately cut, as well. Of course, he asked to see it right away. We are all wondering who would have done such a thing, and why. I have no enemies, so

I can only think it is a kind of mischief, but for reasons which elude me."

"My thoughts and questions are likewise. My father would have done the same as yours if he were here." Abby opened her book to the page she'd read last, marked by a homemade bookmark.

"What are you reading?" Lena leaned forward to have a closer look at the book Abby held.

"*A Daily Rate* by Grace Livingston Hill." Showing her the cover, Abby explained, "It's about a Philadelphia boarding house and a heroine named Celia. I love it so far. In fact, I think it is inspiring my own writing. My first book by this author, but I hope not my last. She writes about characters who believe in the grace and goodness of God. I've not discovered many writers like her, but I love what I've read so far."

"You're a writer?" Lena's smile widened, intrigue evident in her eyes.

Abby nodded. "I am."

"You are so young. May I ask, do you have anything published yet, without sounding as if I am insulting?" Lena chuckled at her question and hurried to add, "I mean, I'm sure you are very talented. I can tell you are an intelligent, warm, caring individual. I'm sure anything you write will be a great success."

"Thank you, yes," Abby replied with a similar chuckle. "I do have a couple of short stories which have been published in some newspapers near my home. That's all so far, however, I deign to admit."

"A great accomplishment, and no small feat. We are both young. I'm sure these victories will spur you on to greater things." Lena leaned back in her chair again.

"What are you reading, if I may ask?" Abby glanced at the open book in her friend's lap.

"*The Longest Journey* by E.M. Forster."

"Do you like it? Is it any good?" Abby inquired. "I've heard of the author but haven't read any of his books yet."

"I like the theme of the novel, and it is well written, but it seems to grow worse as I near the end. The main character chooses to conform with society instead of standing out. The hero isn't much of a hero to me since he is a writer who ends up disappointed in life due to his own faults and poor choices. I cannot recommend anything about it except one should not make the decisions he makes. In my opinion thus far, he only has himself to blame. I'm not a huge fan of E. M. Forster, but it is newly released and has held my attention."

"So your advice to a writer would be not to conform to society's expectations." Abby leaned her head to one side as she considered all her friend had said.

"Right you are. Write about what you believe in, even if society does not. It sounds as though you have convictions of faith, as do I. After reading about this character's fate, I would recommend you do not shy away from writing about your faith."

Abby pondered Lena's words as she stared out at Lake George. The water looked blue again today, but darker than the clear blue sky above. Not a cloud in sight. For miles around, other than the lake, all they could see consisted of majestic pines, fir, and spruce trees topping distant hills; sugar maples; red maples blooming in dark purple hues; ash trees; poplars; a few magnolias here and there; and pin oaks. It did her good to be away from the city and take in the fresh air and sights nature afforded them.

"Lena, you have provided a confirmation to my current and difficult writing endeavor, one which my soul very much needed to hear." Sighing with pleasure, she began reading, more determined than ever to complete her manuscript.

---

*W*ith Lena's words still echoing in her mind as she dressed for dinner, Abby donned one of her favorite frocks, a white evening gown of linen with a layer of organza, a ruffled hem, demi-train, and a blue organza sash at the waist. The gown boasted puffed sleeves, a panel and high-neck collar of lace, and another V-necked, three-inch ruffle dangling above the bodice on the blouse. Elizabeth rolled and pinned her hair up, arranging it in the latest fashion. In turn, Abby helped her sister and Elizabeth with their hair.

Situated in the main dining room at a long table with her family, Abby ordered the lamb with mint sauce accompanied by Hollandaise potatoes, new cauliflower and peas, lettuce with French dressing, and fruit punch. Grandmother ordered *caviar sur canapes* for appetizers and the teal duck with celery and mayonnaise for herself. Catherine debated between the roast veal and broiled bluefish, ultimately choosing the roast veal. Elizabeth settled on Oysters Rockefeller. Two of Gran's fellow book club members, Miss Blanche Lewis and her grandmother, Mrs. Ava Lewis, joined them, and Miss Lena Carter with her parents, Mr. and Mrs. Eugene and Lula Carter, leaving two empty seats.

Abby looked up in surprise when Jack's voice addressed her grandmother at the head of the table. "May we join your table for dinner, ma'am?" Ryan stood at Jack's side, fiddling with his bowtie, looking at Lena and occasionally, Elizabeth.

"Certainly," Gran replied. "We would never turn away two handsome gentlemen from our midst, would we, Ava?"

"Never. Please, have a seat, gentlemen." Mrs. Lewis smiled warmly at their guests as they seated themselves in the vacant chairs across from Abby and Elizabeth.

The heavy chair scraped across the floor, making a bit of a screech as Jack pulled it out, causing him to wince.

Abby smiled. "They are a bit cumbersome, but I've never seen so many beautiful and large, comfortable chairs fit for kings all in one room such as these."

Jack returned her smile. "They are unique, fashioned by local craftsmen. Ornate carvings and high backs. They do make me feel like a king."

"All you need now is to find your queen," Ryan joked as he perused the menu.

"I'm in no hurry." Jack opened his menu. "A search for a queen takes time, and I intend to enjoy the journey."

Clearly. Abby bit her lip to prevent a response to the arrogant nature Jack frequently put forward. Indeed, he seemed to survey everything and every situation. She'd witnessed him in the drawing room observing events from a perch near the fireplace, remaining unusually aloof. Did he evaluate the women as if one might become his future queen?

"A queen with virtues must be carefully selected." Elizabeth reached for her glass of lemonade.

"Surely, not a decision to be rushed. But in addition to what my cousin Elizabeth mentioned, the king must be worthy of the queen's affection." Abby, a smirk playing about her lips at this turn in the discussion, added two cubes of sugar to her steaming teacup and stirred. It wouldn't do to have the gentlemen thinking they were any less selective about their futures when it came to marriage alliances.

"With so many beautiful ladies and handsome gentlemen here, I would not be the least surprised if a great many matches are made at the Sagamore this summer." Grandmother's observation saved the conversation from an uncomfortable lapse. As usual, few things escaped her hearing. Or her insight—such as teaching her granddaughters the playing field between the genders was a level one.

"I highly recommend the roast beef or the broiled fish." Mrs. Ava Lewis wisely turned the topic to food, and Abby could almost hear the number of relieved inward sighs.

"I like the roast veal, myself," Mr. Carter remarked.

After the waitress returned and took more orders, Jack proved himself capable of good manners when he looked down the table and addressed Lena. "I hope you are doing well since the accident, Miss Carter."

"I am much recovered, thank you, Mr. Gable. Abby kept me company on the front porch today while we read wonderful books."

"I hope you won't let this scare keep you from riding in the future, Miss Carter." Ryan accepted a glass of water from the waitress.

"I'm glad you mentioned it. I plan to venture out again next week. My parents and I are signed up to take an island tour in a surrey carriage on Monday. I should be good as new by then." Lena sipped some of her tea. "The camphor oil the infirmary gave me is a wonderful remedy for healing the skin."

"Oh, the island tour in the surrey. Thank you for mentioning it, Lena. I almost forgot to tell my granddaughters I've signed us up for Monday at three o'clock." Grandmother turned to Abigail. "Yes, you'll still have plenty of time for your writing, dear. Everyone, my Abby is a dedicated and disciplined writer working on a novel, so we must forgive her reclusive ways."

"Thank you for thinking of my writing schedule, Gran. I look forward to the island tour." Abby, somewhat embarrassed by Gran's comment, sipped some of her tea as another waiter delivered their appetizer.

"You're a writer like Jack?" Ryan assessed Abby with a raised brow.

Abby nodded. "Yes, but I didn't know Jack is also a writer." No wonder she'd caught him observing everyone and behaving in an aloof manner. Had she misjudged him? Didn't most writers find themselves observing human behavior?

But ... did she behave the same way he did? Of course, she did, if she would admit the truth. It's why her sister and cousin heckled her so much. She lost track of many conversations and events while pondering her next ramblings and writings. Even in a crowded room, she frequently disappeared inside her head to consider a scene, a plot, or some aspect about the science of human behavior and how events could transpire.

"Will you gentlemen be joining in any of the island tours?" Elizabeth tasted some of the caviar.

"I don't know. I haven't given it much thought," Jack answered. "I've taken it before. It's nice."

"I've already seen the island a hundred times over." Ryan shrugged. "I guess I'm an unlikely maybe."

Abby couldn't hide her curiosity any longer. "What kind of writing do you do, Jack?"

"I'm a journalist for *The New York Journal*." Jack slid a cup of black coffee closer toward himself. "I submit pieces about modern-day events and other articles of interest as a freelance writer. If the senior editor likes them, they run them."

"Ah, Hearst is a champion of educating his readers on domestic as well as international affairs, all things I enjoy learning about very much," Grandmother remarked approvingly as she passed the appetizer plate on. "I sometimes read *The New York World*, but Pulitzer likes to publish incessantly about the rights of workers, and I don't own a factory. I do have a few employees, so his paper keeps me informed."

Jack nodded. "That's right. I enjoy everything from domestic to international affairs and current events too. Maybe it's why many of my articles are picked up by *The New York Journal*. Pulitzer's editors rarely have any interest in my work. I do contemplate writing a mystery someday."

While that last pronouncement caught Abby's attention, Catherine toyed with her silverware, looking bored until she chimed in. "Don't let Grandmother fool you. She has several hundred employees. Grandfather owned hotels and restaurants in four states, not to mention her thirty-room estate. Plus, there's the apple orchard which produces apple jelly, apple butter, and many other apple products. It's a factory of sorts, even though it still operates out of a huge, old-fashioned barn. People come from miles around to see it. One day, Abigail will be at the helm of it all. Elizabeth and I shall have our share, of course."

Abby would have kicked Catherine under the table if she could have reached her. All she could do was squeeze her eyes shut and hope no rumors of Grandmother's wealth or her future inheritance would spread. If they did, it could cause an avalanche of unwelcome suitors.

"'Tis merely a humble applesauce facility." Grandmother waved a hand to dismiss the picture her careless granddaughter painted. "We don't want all of those apples to go to waste."

"Of course not, ma'am," Jack replied, doing his best to hide another of his amused smiles as Abby looked away. Then he did a wonderful thing and changed the subject. "My father would prefer I write for Pulitzer because of our investments and employees as well, but it hasn't worked out that way. I like a more generalized approach to journalism. A wide variety of topics and interests turn up in my writing. Lately, for instance, I find myself writing about the state of our economy."

"We need more writers like you, Mr. Gable. Your name does have a familiar ring to it. I believe I've read some of your work." Granny tapped her chin as the waitress brought a rolling cart with their dishes. "Aren't you the one who wrote the article last year about the dangers of the Russian Tsar, who recently restricted his government by legitimizing his right to operate by decree? And the one this past May—which I particularly enjoyed—about Pink Star racing his way through a muddy track to the finish for the win of the thirty-third Kentucky Derby?"

"Yes, I did write those articles. You have an astute memory, Mrs. Wiltshire." Jack straightened in his seat, and his blue eyes twinkled a bit at the mention of some of his work.

"We never miss a Derby, being locals in Kentucky, unless the weather is terrible. Isn't that right, Lula?" Mr. Carter patted his wife's hand.

She nodded with an adoring look at her husband. "Indeed. We look forward to it every year, but this last spring was terribly rainy, hence the mud."

Mr. Carter leaned forward to address Jack. "Speaking of writing about the economy of late, do you have any insight on the copper industry? There are disturbing rumors we've heard, though I must say we aren't big investors in anything except our little horse farm, but some folks are saying to sell before a possible downturn. I have a few friends, however, who might be interested in your thoughts."

"I think you may be hearing good advice, Mr. Carter," Jack replied as the waitress served everyone their salads and main dishes, apologizing about the second course coming out with the main course.

After Mr. Carter offered a prayer for the meal, Abby tuned out the rest of the discussion. She focused on slicing bites of the lamb with mint sauce, savoring the intriguing information about Jackson Gable. A journalist! Could two writers even get along? For a flash of a moment, she pictured the two of them married, living in the same house, both clacking away at their typewriters. The very idea made her chuckle under her breath. How absurd. Then again ...

Halfway through the dinner, the manager, Mr. Alvin Rhodes, stepped before the fireplace at the far end of the hall and clanged a fork against a long-stemmed glass, calling everyone's attention to an announcement he wished to make. Conversations lulled and he proceeded. "Good evening, everyone. We hope you are enjoying your stay at the Sagamore and wish to invite you all to attend a surprise activity this evening which we hope you'll enjoy. Ladies and gentlemen, please join us for an event we call the *Midnight Stargazing Picnic*. Bring a blanket to spread on the lawn for stargazing from eleven to midnight. During this portion of the event, servers will offer our Sagamore guests a complimentary beverage. There will be picnic baskets at the front desk containing deviled eggs, a selection of European chocolates, goat cheese and provolone, gourmet crackers, pickles, olives, and other pickled vegetables, lemon and cheesecake squares, petit fours, and other delightful confections created by our chef and kitchen staff. After the stargazing portion of the evening, which I'm told will be a perfect night with a clear view, the event will culminate with a quarter-of-an-hour fireworks display accompanied by our own sinfonia of musicians as we celebrate the kickoff of summer at Sagamore with illuminations."

The dining room inhabitants burst into applause, followed by a heightened murmur of excitement as Mr. Rhodes bowed and excused himself with a wave. Before the applause diminished, Jack looked at Abby. Shrugging, he exchanged a glance with Ryan, who nodded. They appeared to communicate without words, demonstrating a lengthy friendship. Jack leaned toward Abby and Elizabeth. "Ladies, would you care to join Ryan and me for the *Midnight Stargazing Picnic*? We could meet on the front porch at say, about ten-thirty to choose a good spot on the lawn."

Grandmother nodded and said, "I'm game."

Abby looked at her cousin. "Ten-thirty sounds fine with me. What do you think, Elizabeth?"

"Perfect. We'll be there with quilts and our shawls. It might get chilly." Elizabeth tasted more of her oysters, but no doubt, Abby's cousin hid a great deal of joy behind those down-swept eyelashes of hers. What sounded better than the two of them invited to enjoy a special evening by the gentlemen they had set their affections upon only a week ago? Abby couldn't help but think the good Lord had something to do with the way things unfolded.

Then Ryan spoke up. "We'll be there." And he stared at Elizabeth in such an intense way, Abby squirmed inside for her cousin.

CHAPTER 5

I know I am but summer to your heart, and not the
full four seasons of the year.

— EDNA ST. VINCENT MILLAY

hile Catherine pouted about not
receiving an invitation to stargaze from
Edwin, the boy she adored from afar, Abby changed her
garments, donning a lavender walking dress with long
sleeves and a plum-colored shawl. She suggested
Catherine do them the favor of keeping Grandmother
company on a nearby quilt instead of abandoning her
solely to Blanche and Ava.

"Oh, fine." Catherine sighed. "Perhaps Edwin will
say hello at some point, or some other fellow." She
arranged her hair for the third time.

"You haven't given up on Edwin this soon, have

you?" Abby pinned on a straw hat with a wide white satin ribbon trailing down the back. "Boys of his age are usually shy."

"No, I suppose not entirely." Catherine tucked a curl in place. "Just keeping my options open as you suggested."

"Very good. I'm glad to hear it. I've seen a generous smattering of boys your age here this summer. Surely, one will find his way to your side if your Edwin doesn't realize what perfection you are." Abby glanced at her small collection of jewelry in the case she'd brought along. "Perhaps you'd like to borrow my favorite brooch for the evening. It would look lovely with the high-neck blouse you're wearing."

Her sister perked up, a wide smile appearing on her reflection in the vanity mirror they presently shared. "It certainly would look smart with this outfit. Thank you, Abs."

"You're welcome. I trust you'll return it promptly. It was a—"

"A treasured Christmas gift from Mama," Catherine finished. "I know. I've heard it before. Don't worry. I shan't lose it, and I shall take care to return it this evening before bed."

Abby chuckled. "Good. I think we're ready. Let's sit with Gran and Elizabeth in the sitting room until it's time to join the others. I hear them chatting about how fun tonight will be. Gran is saying she doesn't mind staying up past her bedtime for illuminations."

Not wanting to be fashionably late or too early, their foursome headed downstairs to the foyer to meet Jack and Ryan at precisely twenty minutes after ten o'clock. Gran had chosen to use her cane for the evening's festivities, and Catherine and Abigail each carried a spare quilt. They found Jack and Ryan, both looking handsome and eager to find a location on the lawn, each holding a picnic basket of provisions provided by the staff behind the front desk.

"Ladies, you look beautiful." Jack greeted them first with one of his dashing smiles as Abby paused beside him, and Elizabeth caught up to Ryan.

"Thank you, gentlemen. At my age, I'll take all the compliments I can get," Gran replied, hanging back with Catherine but wearing a sly grin.

Jack grinned in return. He must enjoy Gran's sarcasm.

"Both of you look nice, as well," Elizabeth gushed.

Abby merely nodded, overcome by the intoxicating scent of sandalwood and musk in Jack's cologne. Best not to say too much since his cologne and good looks combined threatened to make her swoon. It wouldn't do to appear lovesick, so she averted her eyes toward guests coming and going in the foyer instead of Mr. Handsome.

"The clerk at the front desk said this basket serves two, and the one Jack has is for four, so we have plenty for all of us," Ryan explained, offering his arm to Elizabeth.

"How nice," Gran replied. "Lead the way and please choose a spot with an excellent view where the sparks won't catch us on fire, bearing in mind we are one-hundred-percent flammable."

Jack chuckled. He'd caught on to Gran's wit. Ryan, on the other hand, only stared at Elizabeth. He might take a tumble if he didn't pay better attention to his path.

"Have I mentioned, you look nearly identical to my great-grandmother when she was your age?" Ryan kept studying Elizabeth while leading them outside into another bevy of action. Employees and musicians scurried to provide the evening's entertainment while guests milled about, selecting locations to spread their blankets.

"She does have a remarkable resemblance to your great-grandmother's portrait," Jack agreed. "I haven't seen it in a few years, but as I recall, they have similar features. Wasn't the portrait in your hotel dining room?"

Ryan nodded. "The portrait is now hanging in our spacious reception room over the stone fireplace. I have convinced Father to market the Grand Forks Hotel and Cottages by reminding everyone of its legacy as one of the oldest lodgings in the Adirondacks."

"How will you go about this excellent idea?" Jack cocked his head.

"I'm going to ask Miss Elizabeth Parker if she will pose alongside the portrait wearing my great-grandmother's elegant shawl. You can write the newspaper article for us, Jack. I'll hire a local photographer from the *Bolton Gazette* to take the photograph." Ryan paused. "That is, if Miss Parker will agree. Once her picture is in all the important newspapers, our legacy will be transformed. Then Grand Forks will return to her former glory."

"What a thrilling invitation! I would be delighted to pose for you—if Grandmother grants her permission, of course." Elizabeth stopped walking and spun around. "You will say yes, won't you, Grandmama?"

"I suppose it won't cause any harm to become a model for a once-in-a-lifetime opportunity." Their grandmother smiled at Elizabeth's pleading face. "All of my granddaughters have the gift of striking and natural beauty. It wouldn't do to hide them from the world, but only one photograph, or your parents might think me a poor excuse for a guardian." She held up a hand. "And only if Jackson, Abigail, and Catherine are present. I possess great fortitude, but not the kind required to row across Lake George and traipse about on an excursion such as that one, which does sound appealing, glamorous, and exciting. But I'm afraid it would wear me out for several days."

"Thank you, thank you, Grandmother!" Elizabeth let go of Ryan's arm to embrace and kiss Gran on her cheek. Gleeful, she spun back around, tucking her hand into her escort's elbow again. "I am so excited about the prospect of this adventure, Ryan. You must tell me everything about your great-grandmother and Grand Forks."

Now they knew a little something about Ryan's local family business. Abby couldn't help but feel a little excitement at the prospect of an additional outing with Jack. Judging by the look on his face, she thought perhaps he looked forward to helping his friend.

Soon, they found a location, spread the quilts, and sat down with what they hoped would result in an ideal view of the stars and the illuminations above. As their eyes adjusted to the darkness, they admired the flickering light of candles in brass containers floating about the serene water of the bathing pool. Elizabeth chatted with Ryan comfortably, and Gran with Catherine until Ava and Blanche joined them, but an awkward silence hung between Abby and Jack. Overcome with a shyness completely unlike herself, she couldn't think of a word to say.

Jack pointed out the Big Dipper and Little Dipper in the stars above, and Abby enjoyed the brush of his shoulder against hers coupled with the visibility of God's handiwork spread out like a quilt over them. Then he sat back, studying her. "I didn't want to put you on the spot at dinner, but if I may ask, I'd love to hear about your writing."

Abby couldn't help but smile. "I'm writing several things, but mainly a memoir about our visit to the West Coast last summer. Grandmother takes us somewhere different each year, and last year, she had her heart set on a visit to California."

"I see. Where in California did you visit?"

"Since Gran's health had been poorly and she'd heard about a healing revival, we went to Los Angeles to attend the Azusa Street Mission and see the Pacific Ocean." Abby studied Jack's face, but she didn't find a readable answer to her question. "Perhaps you've heard of the mission?"

He rubbed his chin. "I have. In fact, I'm curious about it, and having a respect for the faith, find myself somewhat perturbed by accounts I've read. They seem critical and disapproving. How did the visit turn out? What did you think about the mission?"

"It turned out to be life-changing. Grandmother received her healing after numerous doctors had no idea what was wrong. Not only were we profoundly impacted as we witnessed many other miracles, but we were so moved by the power of God demonstrated vividly and vibrantly that we felt called to help with the mission's endeavors. It also spurred me to do my part in spreading the gospel through my writing." She tilted her head toward her sister. "Catherine and I became more dedicated to assisting at our father's parish school where we attended as minister's daughters. As for our cousin, we see her growing spiritual maturity, as if a missing puzzle piece to her faith fell into place."

Jack shifted, pulling a knee to his chest and resting an elbow on it. "I have a quiet but strong faith, though I tried to run from it. One cannot deny miracles like those you've mentioned. I think this is my problem with the other articles I've read about Azusa—I cannot fathom how some writers dare to criticize the mission because of skepticism and what they don't understand."

She pursed her lips. "I agree. I've read some stories about the mission which left me, frankly, indignant. As for my manuscript, I am called to write about Azusa. I have other ideas in synopsis stage, but this piece is the strongest tug on my heart. I must write it first since it won't let go."

He tilted his head. "Memoirs can be challenging to sell, but with a great topic, or if you're a person of fame, they can go like hotcakes."

"I have decided to leave it in God's hands and do what I can to put a solid manuscript together," she confessed. On one hand, it felt good to talk to him about the project, but she also felt vulnerable. What if her book flopped? "The mission is a controversy. Some call it a revival, and others, a spectacle. Even if I don't sell many copies, I will have done what the Lord asked."

His blue eyes twinkling in the lantern light as the musicians tuned their instruments. "My editor would call it a hot topic. He'd want to run it."

She couldn't respond. Had he hinted he would write an article about her book? She didn't want to prey upon her new friendship with him by asking him to pitch her memoir. She didn't know him well enough to ask for such a favor.

"Do you have a title for your memoir?" He leaned back, his arms outstretched behind him, palms down on the quilt to support his strong upper body.

"A title? Yes. I'm simply going to call it *Azusa*."

"*Azusa*," he repeated. "Just the right amount of vague, but informative. I like it."

Elizabeth and Ryan, seated a few feet behind them on the other side of the quilt, held their own quiet conversation about Elizabeth's uncle's general store and hometown of Hamilton, Ohio. They raided the picnic basket for a few snacks as they talked, and a glance at Elizabeth revealed contentment in her expression.

Abby changed the subject with Jack, catching his eye again. "You said you might like to write a mystery. Have you settled on a storyline?"

"I have got this idea about a castle murder mystery. It's kind of sketchy, but it's lurking, pestering me to write it now that I've graduated from law school."

She tilted her head toward him. Many of her ideas stewed and simmered in her mind before she could proceed with writing. "You did mention being away at a university. Where did you attend?"

"Harvard."

"And did they teach you to write mysteries at Harvard?"

He shook his head and chuckled. "Not as much as I wish, but I did take one creative writing class and explored mystery writing in the process. No, I'm afraid I have attained a boring law degree to help Father protect the family assets. In fact, I've been so busy studying for finals and preparing for writing essays to pass the bar, I haven't had time to write many news articles. It's provided a part time means of income, but now I am free to mainly pursue my journalism and writing career."

"You must be relieved to have your law degree. Are you celebrating with this summer retreat in the Sagamore paradise, where inspiration is no more than a glance through the windows?" She waved toward the lake.

"Yes, something like that. Spent a few weeks here every summer, growing up."

"Sounds as though the music is about to begin. Perhaps we can resume this conversation later." Abby's heart fluttered at the prospect of continuing their talk later. The man at her side was far more intriguing than she'd anticipated. He possessed faith. He came from a family of substance. He held an Ivy League law degree. He had established himself as a journalist. He liked mysteries. He had a suave and debonair manner when he didn't flirt with her. He knew how to handle himself around others.

"Certainly. Let's see what's in that picnic basket, shall we?" Jack reached for the handle.

She rubbed her hands together as the sinfonia performed the first few measures of "Swan Lake." "Sounds good. I could do with some dessert."

Jack peeked into the basket. "Pastries and chocolate.

I'd say that calls for a hot drink." Nudging Ryan's back, Jack made as if to get up. "We should make a dash for coffee."

"Oh—no." Abby touched his arm. "I think the illuminations are starting." Several shooting stars whistled and then exploded into gold sprinkles, lighting up the sky. The reverberating thunder of more explosions bursting above them produced enthusiastic clapping from the captivated audience.

Jack settled in so close beside her that their shoulders brushed. Abby reveled in the perfect summer's night, a glorious evening spent in the company of an attractive gentleman offering friendship and stimulating conversation. Might this be the beginning to her best summer yet?

CHAPTER 6

Let beeves and home-bred kine partake the sweets of
Burn-mill meadow; the swan on still St. Mary's Lake
float double, swan and shadow!

— WILLIAM WORDSWORTH

The next morning, Abby followed her family
out of their suite and into the hallway to
head downstairs for breakfast a bit later than usual.
Two uniformed officers, the hotel manager, and two
cleaning ladies employed by the hotel cloistered around
the neighboring suite's open door and part of the hall.
A younger officer directed the cleaning ladies to go
ahead with their tasks and then appeared to jot down
some notes, while the older peered at all those coming
and going. He stepped in front of them, blocking their
way to the staircase and the lift.

"Pardon the interruption, ladies, but I see you reside in the suite next door. We're investigating a crime which occurred here and would like to ask you a few questions." He lifted his officer's cap as he nodded toward the open VanDyne suite. Mrs. VanDyne and her two daughters emerged from the suite after the cleaning ladies rolled their carts inside it at about the same time as Abby and her family approached, heading toward the elevator beyond their neighbor's door.

Mr. Rhodes, the resort manager, turned their way. "Yes, ladies, we would appreciate your help." His mustache twitched as he spoke, his look pleading.

"What seems to be the problem?" Gran asked.

Abby held in a sigh. Her curiosity did not stop the need for a cup of coffee. Couldn't these officers wait until after breakfast? Her eyes had barely cracked open enough to dress, let alone answer questions.

Mrs. Hazel VanDyne crossed her arms over her chest. "We've had a break-in. Our entire suite was ransacked last night during the picnic and fireworks."

"Oh my," Elizabeth breathed, squeezing Abby's hand. "How disturbing! Ransacked!"

Abby perked up, nearly wide awake now. She still wanted coffee, though.

"Indeed. The Bolton police have finally arrived to take a report and investigate the matter." Mrs. VanDyne glanced at the officers with a smirk, evidently displeased they hadn't come calling the night before. Returning her gaze to Grandmother, she added, "Mr.

Rhodes was kind enough to offer us a villa for our safety last night when we returned to our suite and discovered this disaster. We also didn't want to disturb any evidence, so we vacated to the villa with only the barest of necessities. Trust me when I say it was no easy task in the bedlam of what the burglar left."

"How despicable!" Gran gasped. "Please, call me Fanny."

Mrs. VanDyne pinched her lips together. "Thank you, Fanny, and do call me Hazel. The officers have now inspected the disaster. This is Officer Wells and Officer Smith. I'm not sure I would advise you to remain in your suite with three precious young ladies and no gentleman about to protect you, but we're anxious to put this behind us, resume our holiday, and retrieve the remains of our personal possessions."

"The remains of your possessions? Have you determined if anything was stolen?" Gran appeared indignant, drawing herself upright.

The younger daughter, Miss Lillie VanDyne, shook her golden curls. "It's quite a mystery, as our valuables appear to be accounted for, but we can't find some personal papers." Carrie VanDyne, the elder daughter, nodded. Abby had seen Carrie and Lillie around the resort and knew them to be about the same ages as Elizabeth and herself.

The older police officer interrupted the conversation. "We'd simply like to know if you saw or heard anything last night, ladies, since you are next door."

Gran released a chuckle, waving her hand toward Abby and Elizabeth. "Forgive me for laughing, but with these two floating on clouds of joy after being in the presence of two fine gentlemen while we watched the illuminations, an earthquake could have demolished the place and we wouldn't have noticed a thing. We returned to our suite at nearly half past one o'clock in the morning. My granddaughters danced about the sitting room, providing their own rendition of 'Swan Lake' until nearly two, keeping me awake with their *joie de vivre*. I had to contend with a great deal of giggling, chatter, singing, and twirling about our sitting room. In short, officer, we didn't see or hear a thing apart from my granddaughters carrying on."

Gran earned a smile from the officer after he glanced at Elizabeth and Abby, craning his neck to have a look at Catherine. "I see. I'm Officer Smith, by the way." He shook hands with Gran. The other officer paused from taking notes to introduce himself as Officer Wells.

Abby shifted her weight to her other foot. True, they had danced about the sitting room a bit. The evening would forever live on in her mind as one of the most romantic she'd enjoyed, minus kissing. They didn't know Jack or Ryan well enough to engage in a kiss, but otherwise, she held dear memories of sweet conversation, amorous glances, and enjoying a picnic basket full of delectable treats against the backdrop of entertaining music and fireworks bursting in the night sky. Still ...

did Gran have to make them sound like lovesick puppies?

If she had to guess, her relationship with Jack did seem promising, but she'd make herself scarce today and take things slow. She'd spent much of the early morning hours asking herself a question. If she let Jack become part of her life, would he clip her wings or enable her to soar? As a writer himself, surely, he would never expect her to give up her love for the same art, as an ordinary gentleman might insist upon after marriage. Didn't most men want subservient wives who spent hours in the kitchen and provided them with offspring? Offspring she would also need to look after. Would Jack respect her need to continue to write even if she became a wife and mother? Maybe he would prove himself different.

She really could use a cup of steaming hot coffee before wrestling with these reoccurring thoughts.

But the younger officer wasn't quite finished. He scribbled something on his notepad and cocked a brow at Gran. "And your name is ..."

"Wiltshire. Mrs. Fanny Goldman Wiltshire. I wish we could offer something more useful, however. The unresolved nature of this situation makes me concerned for our safety," Gran remarked.

"When you say you watched the fireworks display with two gentlemen, were you all together the entire evening?" Officer Smith inquired while Officer Wells poised himself to write down more notes.

Under her skirt, Abby tapped the toe of her boot. Did the police intend to question everyone on Green Island, or just those on the floor with the VanDyne suite? Perhaps he would question employees too. Staff had keys, after all.

"With the exception of the gentlemen leaving for a short while to find us some strong coffee and the usual powder room breaks, yes, we were together the entire time," Grandmother replied. "Goodness, perhaps we should move to a villa after breakfast, Mr. Rhodes."

The younger Officer Wells jotted down more notes.

The mention of coffee made her stomach rumble, but Abby bit her tongue and prayed for patience.

"And the names of your escorts?" Officer Smith wanted details.

When Gran's alert expression melted into a faraway stare and she tapped her chin, Abby stepped forward. "I'm certain they are innocent regarding this matter, but one is named Ryan. I don't remember his last name. The other is named Jack. Jackson Gable. He's an attorney-at-law. I highly doubt he would jeopardize his good name with actions of this kind."

Officer Wells scribbled down the names.

"Ryan's last name is Steele." Elizabeth lifted her chin as she spoke up. "His father owns the Grand Forks Hotel and Cottages across from Green Island. I'm sure he wouldn't be mixed up in something like this either."

"When can you show us a villa, Mr. Rhodes?" Tone

tinged with impatience, Grandmother loosened, then tightened her grip on her cane.

"Have no fear, Mrs. Wiltshire." Despite his choice of words, Mr. Rhodes's voice shook. "I plan to double our security. I assure all of you, the matter is well in hand. The Sagamore prides itself in looking after our guests. We will get to the bottom of this. If you would like me to see if we have another vacancy, I'll do my best as soon as the officers finish their investigation."

Mrs. VanDyne clucked her tongue. "I'm not so sure about the matter being well in hand. My jewels appear to be safe, and we're alive, but at the very least, my personal correspondence has vanished. I can't imagine what someone would want with letters to my mother and dear friends of ours."

"Your family is known in all the right circles in New York and Boston. Someone could be targeting your close acquaintances and friends to obtain a profit in some way. People like us would never think of such a method." Grandmother tapped her cane on the floor for emphasis. "No, people like us, we invite society to elaborate dinners, soirees, luncheons, fundraising events, and afternoon tea. We entertain first, and then we are forthright and ask our friends and acquaintances to join us in our ventures. We go about it in an altogether more direct and upright manner, making it nearly offensive to refuse, but others of a different caliber might stoop to thievery to obtain names and addresses to solicit, steal from, coerce, or blackmail our unsuspecting friends in an altogether devious way."

Mrs. VanDyne gulped at Gran's words. Like Abby, she found a chuckle at something in what Gran had said despite her current circumstance. "How right you are. We do go about it in a much more upright manner. We entertain our friends before taking their money. Thank you, Mrs. Wiltshire. I needed the laugh this morning."

"Glad to cheer you up. Hopefully, nothing else is missing other than some letters and papers. Do you have your address book? Is your suite a terrible mess?"

"A horrifying mess," Hazel replied, shuddering. "Things knocked to the ground in every room, vases of fresh flowers spilled, drawers overturned and the contents strewn about. The maids will take hours to put it to rights. Maybe days, even. As for my address book, that's an astute question. I'm not sure if it's here now that you mention it. Lillie, darling, step inside and see if you can find it. You know where I keep it."

"Yes, Mama. I'll look." Miss Lillie bobbed a compliant curtsy to her mother and glanced toward the officers. They consented with nods, and she ducked inside the suite.

"I'm so sorry." Gran sighed. "Let us know if there is anything we can do for you. Mr. Rhodes, I look forward to hearing from you at your soonest convenience, and certainly well before dinner."

Mr. Rhodes placed his hands behind his back and offered a curt nod. "Yes, Mrs. Wiltshire."

"Dreadful situation," Elizabeth murmured in Abby's ear. Abby nodded.

Miss Carrie VanDyne held her mother's hand, a look of distress visible on her usually calm and serene face. "Thank you, Mrs. Wiltshire. It's very comforting to know we have friends we can count on in this situation. Mama is beside herself."

Mrs. VanDyne held a hand to her temple, but after a moment, she recovered her composure. "Pardon me for forgetting my manners amid this catastrophe. Do drop in for tea at our villa when we've settled. Bring your lovely granddaughters. Thank you for assisting the officers with their questions."

"Of course. In the meantime, I hope you can get some rest. I'm sure the staff at the Sagamore will restore order speedily." Gran returned a sympathetic look.

"Make sure your suite is locked at all times, ladies," Officer Smith advised.

"We certainly will," Abby replied when Grandmother bit her lower lip and delayed a response, no doubt digesting the disturbance to the comfortable routine they'd settled into.

Miss Lillie reappeared. "It's gone, Mama. It's not there. I checked every drawer in the desk. It's not on the floor either."

"Oh, dear me. All our addresses, missing! I know we locked our suite when we went to the picnic. Whoever did this obviously picked our lock or had a key." Mrs. VanDyne closed her eyes and leaned against the door-frame, her hand returning to her forehead. "Someone can have a riot of a soiree with the names in my address book. My husband will simply be horrified when he is able to join us here. Some business matters he had to attend have delayed him joining us. In fact, he may never let us return in the future if we cannot recover our missing papers. I don't wonder if we won't find something else missing."

"I do hope they are recovered. Come along, girls. We'd better get out of the way and let the officers finish conducting their investigation." Grandmother led them to the lift, and they entered in silence.

First, Abby needed coffee and something in her stomach, which was now growling at regular intervals, demanding nourishment. Then she could take a brisk turn about the lawn and clear her head with some fresh air and prayer. The Lord would either supply them with the resolve to stay in their suite or the wisdom to transfer to a villa.

CHAPTER 7

You know my methods, Watson.

— SIR ARTHUR CONAN DOYLE, *THE MEMOIRS OF SHERLOCK HOLMES* (1893)

*T*here would be no writing for Abby as they settled into a two-story villa Mr. Rhodes secured for them, much to Gran's openly expressed relief. He graciously spared a bellhop, several maids, and a cart and mule to assist with the transfer of their belongings. Their trunks repacked haphazardly, everyone lugged an armful of items across the lawn, allowing Gran to ride on the loaded cart beside the driver while holding onto her hat. Abby had tied a wide, folded white scarf over her hat and beneath her chin so she didn't have to worry about keeping the hat atop her head in the afternoon breeze as she carried her typewriter to the villa, her manuscript bound with a single pale-pink ribbon and tucked safely under her other arm. With a thief who took letters, she didn't trust anyone else to move her manuscript.

The idea of moving hadn't appealed to any of them, but after touring the villa, Grandmother had promised Abby the extra bedroom. Elizabeth and Catherine had seemed pleased to share a bedroom for a change of pace. Abby loved the idea of less interruptions for her writing.

The spacious villa had two bedrooms and a powder room with a bear-claw bathing tub upstairs. The hallway joining the two bedrooms upstairs led to a small balcony on the second floor, facing the rear. It offered a lovely view of the stables, a meadow, and a wooded area. Downstairs, a much larger sitting room with a fireplace occupied most of the center of the main floor, with a small dining room to one side, a galley kitchenette off the entrance hall, and a master bedroom with its own powder room and porcelain bathing tub. Abby could hardly wait to soak in one of those tubs.

They would enjoy the private, covered terrace off the sitting room—with its round dining table, potted plants and ferns, and gabled, green-shingled roof upheld by two Greco-Roman columns. Mr. Rhodes even went so far as to have a fourth chaise lounge sent over so they could all relax and bask in the excellent view of Lake George at the same time.

After the girls settled into the upstairs bedrooms

and Grandmother into the master, unpacked their items, and adjusted to the longer walks to the dining room for meals, they attended church on Sunday at the little white chapel on the southeast corner of the island. Abby hoped to find Jack there since he'd alluded to his faith, but her expectant heart took a tumble when he didn't appear. She did her best not to puzzle over his absence during the sermon. They hadn't seen hide nor hair of him or Ryan since the night of the illuminations, not even at meals.

Perhaps Jack had decided to order meals and have them delivered to his accommodations. Perhaps he'd come down with a summer cold. She hadn't asked if he roomed in the main house or somewhere else, but it was also possible that like most writers, he'd disappeared to make progress with his newspaper articles. Maybe he'd even started writing his murder mystery. She wasn't alone in her unease. Elizabeth had begun to pine for Ryan, but Catherine reassured her by suggesting he likely had responsibilities to tend at Grand Forks Hotel and Cottages.

Meanwhile, the officers continued to poke around the property, interviewing guests throughout the weekend, and nearly every encounter with anyone in one of the dining rooms or around the Sagamore led to a discussion about the VanDynes' "ransacking."

By Monday afternoon, excitement about the island tour settled on their party. Abby and her sister and cousin had gone horseback riding and walking around much of the island, but they had yet to explore all of it.

Abby chose the rear seat of the surrey where her taller height shouldn't obstruct anyone else's view. She'd worn her white scarf over her straw hat, tied beneath her chin in a lovely, albeit enormous bow, and an olive-green shawl over her long-sleeved, pigeon-front white blouse. Catherine, true to her word, had returned her brooch, the only adornment on Abby's high-neck lace collar. The blouse and shawl paired nicely with her long white cotton skirt and wrist-length gloves. Elizabeth sat beside her, then Catherine squeezed in, and on the outside edge, Grandmother took the last space in the row.

When a familiar-sounding cough came from the gentleman next to her, Abby looked up from arranging her skirts. The man lowered the newspaper he'd held open at eye level.

Catching sight of an unmistakable pair of twinkling blue eyes returning her glance with an arrogant smile and upward tilt of a strong nose and jawline, Abby spoke barely above a whisper. "Jack?"

Was he wearing a fake mustache? And why on earth was he sporting a tweed cloak with a cape in this summer-shawl weather? While the cloudy day seemed a little chillier than usual, frequent warm breezes blew from the lake over the island. Her extra layer of petti-coat and stockings left her slightly warm and uncom-fortable, so she couldn't imagine wearing such a long, heavy cloak. A tweed beanie rested on Jack's head with an abbreviated brim and flaps covering his ears.

The mustache did not cling as it should and slipped over his upper lip in a crooked manner. Abby chuckled. She loved Sir Arthur Conan Doyle's stories as much as Jack obviously did. She could hardly contain her amusement as the surrey driver snapped the reins and the fully loaded conveyance lurched forward.

Jack took on a serious look, and he turned the page of the newspaper before giving Abby another grin, this one less arrogant. He pressed a finger to his lips.

Abby defied his request with another snicker. She couldn't help it. "Jack, what are you doing in that get-up? And wherever did you find it? Or should I say, *Sherlock*?"

The companions in her row overheard her whispered questions. They leaned forward and peered at him, taking in his delightful costume.

"Hello, Jack," Fanny said without any attempt to lower her voice whatsoever.

Jack almost visibly melted as he rolled his eyes, keeping his face forward.

"Nice to see you, Jack," Elizabeth whispered.

"It's good to see you again, Jack," Catherine added.

Jack cleared his throat and pressed his mustache into place. His voice controlled and low, he replied, "It's nice to see you all too." He resumed reading the newspaper, hiding behind it, occasionally glancing about over its top edge.

Abby leaned close and whispered, "I take it you're investigating something. I'd venture to guess you've been riding the surrey for more than one tour, and it's the horseback riding accident and the VanDynes' ransacking which has you in mystery-solving mode. As for the disguise, I'll guess you found it in the bottom of some closet of costumes left over from a theatrical performance hosted by the Sagamore in previous years. Next to the Cleopatra costume, I presume."

Jack's blue eyes widened. "You've discovered the costume closet?"

She chuckled, nodding. "I accidentally opened the same closet door when exploring some of the main rooms in the hotel last week. I thought it led to another dining room, but lo and behold, all sorts of costumes and props. I particularly enjoyed the tiara and pink satin princess gown. Did you happen to see the Queen Victoria fur robes, velvet crown, and royal diadem?"

"I did," he replied, turning the page of his newspaper as the tour guide stood and turned around to face the passengers. She extended her arm toward the boathouse ahead on their left and gave a few words about the location as the surrey driver halted the horses.

"Have you found any clues?" Abby inquired when the hostess finished speaking.

When the surrey lurched forward, Jack leaned toward her. "Absolutely nothing. Would you mind if I joined you and your family for dinner this evening?

Perhaps after dinner we could take a brief stroll and put our heads together. You know, go over the facts of what we do know."

"Certainly." Abby hid a smile. So her "mystery man and beau to adore from afar" hadn't completely fallen off the face of the earth, after all. "As for facts, I think we shall have to pray for revelation."

Jack stared at her as if the idea of prayer hadn't occurred to him. "Elementary, my dear. Elementary!"

His remark made her chuckle, but the way he looked at her gave pause for concern. She prayed for everything, especially when she needed answers. Didn't everyone? No, she supposed they did not, but it seldom failed her. The Holy Spirit usually led her to the answers she needed. She'd prayed yesterday at church with bowed head and again during her devotional that very morning for the perpetrator of these crimes to be hindered, caught, stopped, and reformed—even saved by the same merciful grace the Lord Jesus had given her. 'Twas no doubt a grace she didn't deserve, but who did? The Word said all men had fallen short of the glory of God. All of mankind needed grace, mercy, and salvation, and the Lord gave it freely to anyone who asked and believed on His name.

Soon, the tour came to an end. Jack jumped out, and flinging one corner of his cape over a shoulder when he landed, held his hand up to assist her like a perfect gentleman. While she found him attractive on many levels, Abby reminded herself she had arrived on Green

Island with absolutely no intention of falling in love. No, she intended to content herself with as much writing as possible, not tie herself down to anyone. Still, Jack intrigued her. Could she have both freedom and love in one package?

CHAPTER 8

And I saw that all toil and all achievement spring
from one person's envy of another. This too is mean-
ingless, a chasing after the wind.

— ECCLESIASTES 4:4

*J*ack leaned back in his chair at dinner in
the Sagamore's luxurious main dining
room. Seated directly across from Miss
Abigail Greenwood, he could relish her radiant smile
framed by chocolate-colored eyes and hair, contrasting
with her creamy-smooth complexion and perfectly
balanced, delicate features. He had the best view in the
main house.

Abby struck him as a complex creature made up of
many paradoxes. Independent and strong, yet he
detected her fragile slender frame and her youth,

guessing she wouldn't recognize a need to be looked after in a world where predators and danger existed. Intelligent, steadfast, sultry, and innocent—all words he could use to describe Miss Abigail Greenwood. Filled with admirable faith and devotion to God, but trapped in a world where crime and injustice could occur— trapped like himself. Only, creatures like Abby didn't belong there. She was too pure and good for the harsh world.

In the short time he'd known her, he had observed she possessed a way of hovering about like a butterfly, but ready to take flight if needed. Cautious. He liked that in a person. Most of all, he liked her confidence coupled with a sensible, humble nature.

Someone handed him a pepper shaker, and he stared at it. Might he escort her to Friday's dance? Or would the invitation scare her away? Would he first need to ask her grandmother's permission or declare his long-term intentions with Fanny Wiltshire's grand-daughter?

"Pass it to Mrs. Carter." Mrs. Wiltshire herself elbowed Jack gently.

"Pardon?"

"The pepper shaker." She chuckled and nodded toward the object he held.

"Oh, yes, of course." Jack handed the pepper shaker to Mrs. Carter. How nice of the family to join them at dinner again. He enjoyed Mr. Carter's banter about horses and all things Kentucky. Judging by her rosy cheeks and smile, Miss Carter had fully recovered since her fall. She moved around the resort with ease now.

His attention immediately returned to the beautiful Abigail. How had she turned him into a captive of her charms? He'd had no intention of allowing any such thing this summer. No, he only wanted to unwind after having made it through law school, yet here he sat, dreaming of every complexity and nuance of Miss Abigail Greenwood.

"How is your roast beef?" Abby stared at him with those lovely brown eyes, her face like an angel's. She had such peace hovering about her. Did she know?

"My roast beef? Splendid. It has good flavor and it's tender. Just the way I like it. I haven't tried the lima beans or cabbage yet, but Mother would be proud of me for ordering vegetables." He paused. At his age, he shouldn't have mentioned vegetables and mother in the same sentence. He needed to recover. "How is your chicken cacciatore?"

"Delicious. Please, help yourself to some of my asparagus on toast. With this much pasta, I know I won't finish it." Abby slid the side dish toward him. "Asparagus done right is something to write home about."

"Indeed." Jack chuckled. Sagamore's asparagus on toast made his mother happy too. In fact, his mother would probably love Abby. They had much in common. If he had to describe Abby to his mother in his next letter, he'd write: *Dear Mother, You'll find Abby fashion-*

able, independent, smart, friendly, spunky, and filled with faith. All the things I love about you. He'd sign his name as Jackson with a flourish and send it off in the next post. Then he shook his head to clear his mind and sliced more of his roast beef. Where in the world was that tomato bisque he'd ordered?

A discussion between Elizabeth and Catherine began about saving room for the assorted pies and cakes listed on the menu card, drawing everyone's attention to the dessert table. Apple, cherry, blueberry, pecan, and peach pie flavors awaited them along with lemon, strawberry, and white cake.

A waiter appeared with a large tray containing their cups of tomato bisque and a few side salads. Again, he apologized for bringing the first course out after the main course.

"It's all right," Mr. Carter assured him. "We know it's busy in the kitchen. The extra complimentary rolls and butter make up for it."

Nearly everyone had ordered the tomato bisque except for Miss Elizabeth Parker, Mrs. Ava Lewis, and Miss Blanche Lewis. Jack passed their romaine lettuce side salads to them when they came his way through Mrs. Carter, and to the others cups of soup, including himself. The waiter placed another basket of rolls on the table, causing Mr. Carter to smile. Then the fellow took more of the soup to the next table.

A few moments later, someone began coughing and choking at the table behind theirs, and Jack twisted around in his seat to see what had caused the matter. The man reached for a glass of water. He must've eaten something too spicy. However, when Jack turned to face Abigail again, she and Catherine began coughing.

"S-salty! Too much ... salt," Abby managed to choke out, pushing her cup of soup away and reaching for her water glass.

Jack sipped some of his soup, as did Mrs. Wiltshire. Their mouths twisted. Far too salty.

"Oh, dear me. This is terrible! Didn't the chef taste the food?" Lula Carter sputtered. "So unlike the Sagamore."

Mrs. Wiltshire shook her head. "Such a disappointment."

"They've held an impeccable reputation—until this year. They have much to make up for. Horseback riding accidents, security issues, and now the food. Maybe they need new management," Ava Lewis remarked.

Jack's brows furrowed. He'd overheard similar sentiments expressed by others about the place. It made him more determined to get to the bottom of the odd incidents. He hadn't shared with those in his company that his father sat on the board of investors, but if problems continued, harm would come to the Sagamore, tarnishing its standing in society, and ultimately, profitability.

Others around the dining hall began to cough and sputter in like manner, and the servers soon caught wind of the mishap. They dashed about collecting the cups and bowls of salty tomato bisque, returning a while later to offer patrons bowls of vegetable beef soup or side salads instead. Next, Mr. Rhodes appeared with the chef, visiting each table to offer free desserts as an apology. The chef looked bewildered, stumbling over his words. Mr. Rhodes had a nervous twitch in his mustache and beads of sweat forming on his forehead.

Jack felt sorry for them, but he withheld comment. At this point, sabotage or accidental error could have caused the error. Everyone soon recovered, and pleasant banter began once again, leaving them free to begin the dessert course.

"There you are, Ryan," Elizabeth said when his friend sauntered into the dining room and joined them, landing in one of the vacant seats. "We've missed you these past few days. How've you been?"

"Sorry I'm late, everyone. I've been helping Father at Grand Forks," he explained. "We had a surge in guests, and then I couldn't get away."

"Ryan. Good to see you." Jack tilted his head in his direction. "Extra guests are good for business."

Ryan nodded. "Sure are. Good to see you too." He paused, studying Elizabeth. "I'm anxious to make the arrangements for the photograph of Miss Parker wearing my great-grandmother's shawl. Would you care for an evening horseback ride to discuss it, Miss Parker? I've spoken with the stable and checked the saddle myself for your safety, and some of our other acquaintances are out riding, so we won't be unchaperoned."

His brow rose, indicating his hope in her answer. The shiny new riding boots he wore with his navy sport coat, tan riding breeches, and white shirt hinted that Ryan had dressed to impress Abby's cousin.

"I'd love to go riding and discuss the photograph." Elizabeth toyed with the pearl bracelet on her wrist. "In fact, I've been trying my hair in different styles and wanted to ask about your grandmother's hairstyle in the portrait. If it's all right with Gran, an evening ride sounds perfect."

Abby had finished the last of her pie and most of her coffee. Jack leaned her way. "Would you care for a stroll on the portico, Abby?"

"Fresh air would do me wonders." Abby sipped more of her coffee and returned her cup to the saucer, looking at Mrs. Wiltshire for approval.

"It's fine with me, girls. Catherine can escort me to the villa. Don't be gone too long. Something is amiss at the Sagamore, and I can't put my finger on it. I trust you gentlemen will have my granddaughters delivered safely to our villa just after sunset, by dark." Mrs. Wiltshire consulted the timepiece pinned to her elaborate, shimmering evening gown. "That gives you precisely fifty minutes in case you're wondering exactly what I meant. I know there are workers at the stable to keep an eye on you there, and plenty of activity around the portico. I trust you won't need any other chaperoning."

"I'll have Miss Abigail Greenwood delivered safely and promptly," Jack assured as he stood and made his way down the aisle to the head of the table where he met a smiling Abigail and held out his arm for her. Ryan confidently echoed his words regarding Miss Parker, but Jack could feel Fanny Wiltshire's stare all the way to the French doors leading onto the portico.

CHAPTER 9

Let my heart be still a moment and this mystery explore...

— EDGAR ALLEN POE

*R*yan escorted Elizabeth on their heels through the same set of doors, but they turned left and headed around the corner toward the stable while Jack strolled with Abby to the right. Stepping out onto the colonnade felt like stepping into a wonderland beneath the fading sunshine of a golden evening, bright lantern lighting, and the outdoor chandeliers dangling above. As they walked, he relished the feel of her hand on his forearm, and the fact they had the length of the portico running alongside one wing of the Sagamore to themselves. Even with no others in sight, as Mrs. Wiltshire had said, no one could consider anyone truly alone with so many long windows and sets of French doors offering light and visibility from the dining room.

"Jack, I must tell you," Abby began, "I have a terrible feeling we should go look for clues around the rear kitchen entrance. Someone may have sabotaged the soup."

"Maybe so," he replied.

"I was dressed and ready for dinner early this evening, reading my Bible on the terrace with a cup of tea with Gran. It was so nice and very relaxing after our island tour this afternoon. But you'll never guess the verse the Lord led me to read. Matthew chapter five, verse thirteen. 'Ye are the salt of the earth: but if the salt have lost his savor, wherewith shall it be salted? It is thenceforth good for nothing, but to be cast out, and to be trodden under foot of men.'"

Jack frowned. "Yes. I know the verse."

"Don't you see? With the mention of salt and feet, I think the Lord is telling us to pay attention. Someone wreaking havoc on the place kind of goes with the 'trodden under foot' and 'casting out' part. Maybe this person has lost their way or never found their way to be doing these kinds of things, you know? He or she needs restoration, and sometimes the only way to find it is when the administration of justice brings about true repentance." Abby gave him an imploring glance. "I very much think any evidence we might find will soon be gone if we do not hurry."

"All right, all right, I don't think we'll find anything, but if it will make you feel better, let's have a quick look around. But then we'll return here and finish our walk. I want to save time to pool the facts we do know," he explained.

She nodded, swinging around with him to face the opposite direction. "Agreed. Please, lead the way."

After they rounded the corner and crossed to the rear of the main house, they passed beyond the next corner, arriving at the kitchen garden on their right and the servants' entrance to the kitchen on their left. Jack studied the ground for tracks around the trash and waste bin area, but his earlier assumption that clues would be in short supply proved correct. Far too many employees took waste out of the main house and villas throughout each day.

Abby lingered in front of the door stoop with her hands on her hips. The short walkway ended at a graveled area, dissipating into the hard-packed earth around the gated waste bin. Something caught her eye to the right, and she beckoned him to her side. "Look, Jack. I hate to say it, but tell me those aren't riding boot tracks in the mud leading to the pump." She pointed at a set of tracks leading to the red water pump. The gravel had worn away, likely from the kitchen crew tossing so much liquid waste in the spot. The mud had even splashed the stucco of the main structure. "Those aren't footprints made by typical work shoes or walking shoes. Those are most likely from men's riding boots, are they not? They have a heel and a rounded toe, and they are larger than most women's feet."

Jack squatted and inspected the tracks carefully. They led to the pump and then disappeared where the grass began on the other side. And could the white flecks in the first few actually be table salt?

He flicked away a few remaining pieces of gravel and identified another footprint, most likely belonging to a female employee. It had a small heel, seemed narrower, and had left a pointed tip impression in the mud. One more print appeared completely different, more like a work shoe belonging to a man. These two individuals had walked along the drier edge, telling him someone accustomed to the mud had tried to avoid the area.

He stood up and after another look around, glanced at Abby, extending his hand. "Let's return and discuss this on our walk."

She nodded, slipping her hand in his outstretched one.

Under the portico, they slowed their pace, walking hand in hand, comfortable in the silence. He enjoyed the feel of her slender, smaller hand in his larger one. After a while, they stopped holding hands as if to signal the beginning of a serious discussion.

"What do we know so far?" Abby looked beautiful as she asked the question, but did he dare tell her such a thing yet?

Jack peered down at the ground as they walked to

focus his mind. "The saddle strap was cut, in my opinion, but I can't find any connection between Miss Lena Carter and the VanDynes' ransacking to indicate an attempt to harm any certain person or family. I think we can rule out an intention to murder, for the moment."

"All right. Another point to consider." She turned around to face him, clasping her hands behind her back and walking backwards playfully. "I'm not sure if you've heard, but Hazel VanDyne said her address book was stolen along with some letters from her desk. The thief left her jewels alone, but it doesn't mean they weren't targeted. They may have been in a safe, and perhaps the thief failed to open it."

"Good point. I did hear something along those lines. News travels fast around here." Jack raked a hand through his hair. He hoped she wouldn't run into the brass container of ferns up ahead. "Most of the suites have a safe. And the salt incident could have been an unrelated accident made by someone among the kitchen staff."

"I agree, but I am disturbed about those footprints. Ryan showed up late for dinner and wearing riding boots. I didn't get a good look at them, but you may have since he sat on your side of the table." Abby spun around to face forward again, just in time to avoid a collision with those ferns. "I hate to ask since he's your friend, but were they rounded?"

He shrugged. "The rounded prints could be Ryan's, but maybe they belong to someone else. Or he could've stepped in a muddy bank on the island and went around to the pump to clean them off before coming inside. Maybe he even decided to pop into the kitchen and say hello to the staff. Growing up around here, he knows everyone. It's not unusual for him to go inside and have a taste of something, greet the chef, and cause a great distraction in the kitchen. He could have even stepped in some spilled salt."

"And the other tracks?" Abby's brow rose.

"I think they match the typical work shoes the Sagamore staff uniforms require, which means very little. That all said, I think Ryan was the only gentleman at dinner wearing riding boots this evening, but who knows? The dining room was full. I wasn't looking around at what everyone wore. It's not enough evidence to connect him to the soup disaster, in my opinion. It only places him in the vicinity around or shortly after the incident."

She nodded. "Okay, but is Ryan capable of these other incidents? I thought he was with you the whole time on the night of the ransacking."

Jack evaded her gaze. "Well, not exactly. When we went looking for coffee and to use the necessary in the main house, he went after the coffee while I ended up talking to an acquaintance in the drawing room, Everett Peterson. He's a successful wheat and dairy farmer from New York. He was waiting for someone, but I'm not sure who. Maybe one of his sisters went upstairs to freshen up. I remember thinking Ryan had been missing a long time. I guess it's even possible Ryan could have gone upstairs and then slipped past me when he came back down. When I saw him next, he came from the direction of the kitchen and main dining room."

"Hmm." She processed that as they reached the end of the portico and sat down on a bench together. "What motive could he have if he's behind these crazy incidents? I mean, he's probably innocent, but I've noticed he goes riding frequently, so he could easily gain access to the stable and the tack to have damaged that sidesaddle. He knows the staff well enough to figure out where to find the keys to a room. He was here the day of the horseback riding incident. He was here the night of the ransacking, and again tonight, appearing almost immediately after the soup incident. He could easily slip in and out of the kitchen if employees are busy and accustomed to his presence. All he'd have to do is walk in and out of the back kitchen door, right?"

Jack nodded, leaning forward, interlocking his hands and staring at them. "Yes, you're right. As for motive, I don't know. I hate to think he would do these things for *any* reason. I'm not sure what his motive could be other than to make the Sagamore look bad in hopes more people would stay at his father's hotel, but I've never known him to be so vindictive or to consider such drastic measures. Maybe they're struggling more than I realize. It is all puzzling to me. I've grown up with him, and he's always been a good friend. He does seem quieter than usual this year, however."

Abby rested her hand on his forearm. "I sincerely hope we are wrong. I don't know much about him, but for your sake and the sake of my cousin, I pray we are dead wrong."

He sighed. "I hope so too. I really do."

"Another thing, Jack. I'm worried about the U.S. ambassador to Belgium and France staying here at present. He brought his wife, two daughters, and son. The party arrived over the weekend, you know. Gran saw them briefly after church. One of the ambassador's daughters will be attending the debutante ball in New York, according to my grandmother. She heard about it directly from the ambassador's wife, Ellen. I suggest we keep our eyes on Mr. Archibald Gardmont and his family. They are very kind and well respected. I would feel terrible if something happened to them."

"Indeed. Not to mention, it would draw international attention to the incident, and the perpetrator would be forever destroyed." Jack shuddered, then crossed his arms.

"Have you met the ambassador's two daughters, Miss Willa Gardmont and Miss Daisey Gardmont? They have a son, also. My grandmother is tremendously happy they are here. She met the ambassador and his wife some years ago at a society ball in New York."

He shook his head. "No, I haven't met the ambassador or his family yet. I do know a senator from Wisconsin is here, and I overheard the clerk at the front desk say an earl is arriving from England any day now."

"An earl? How exciting!" Abby smiled.

"Yes. I believe the clerk said he is traveling with his wealthy New York relation, Tybalt Monroe. A cousin, I think. Monroe's father is a successful cattle rancher from Texas. He sent Tybalt to live in New York to cater to their clients there, most of whom represent fine dining and hotel establishments. He sells their beef to places like Delmonico's."

"Ah, I see. Do you know the name of this earl?" Abby paused to pluck a wild violet from the lawn.

"It's a long name. Let me see if I can remember." He squinted. "I believe it is Lord Quinton Bailey Monroe, the Earl of Bloxham-Carlisle."

"My goodness, that is a dreadfully long name and title. Well done, Jack." She chuckled, tucking the violet in some strands of her hair.

He straightened, uncrossing his arms. "As for Ryan, it's hard for me to believe he could be connected to any of this, but I could ask him how things are going. If he's having problems, maybe he'll confide in me. I can't think why else he'd do any of these things except to help his father's business gain an advantage over the Sagamore. It would be out of character for him to stoop to these kinds of tactics, but I won't pretend to be so naïve as to think it's not possible."

Abby glanced at the timepiece pinned to the bodice of her dress. "Excellent. Now you'd best escort me home, Sherlock. We have about ten minutes to reach my villa before sunset. If we are late, Grandmother will never let you escort me anywhere ever again."

"Yes, of course," he said, retrieving her hand and drawing it to his lips. He kissed the back of it, taking her by surprise. "I've enjoyed our time together this evening, Miss Greenwood."

"As have I, Mr. Gable."

CHAPTER 10

Seeking for happiness we must go slowly; the road leads not down avenues of haste; but often gently winds through by ways lowly, whose hidden pleasures are serene and chaste. Seeking for happiness we must take heed of simple joys that are not found in speed.

— ELLA WHEELER WILCOX, "SEEKING FOR HAPPINESS"

The whirlwind arrival of the senator and his family, the ambassador and his family, the cattle tycoon's son, and the earl stirred things up considerably, but no more so for Abigail than the arrival of Miss Augusta Herman. The eighteen-year-old architect's daughter from New York arrived during a storm, bringing the thundering weather to Sagamore along with her *nouveau riche* family, as some referred to them. Miss Augusta's family members included an older sister —Miss Isadora Herman, nineteen—and their parents, Peter and Lucy Herman.

Abby and her family, on the way to breakfast, had occasion to observe the latest arrivals. Checking in at the front desk, Augusta caught everyone's attention in the grand foyer when she insisted the Sagamore relinquish someone from their staff to be her personal maid throughout her stay, since her own maid—she informed the clerk—had come down with some sort of ailment and had cancelled the journey at the last moment.

Miss Augusta's voice had a kind of shrill sound to it when she gave her demands, and this in and of itself gave Abby, Elizabeth, Catherine, and Grandmother equal pause. With their skirts and umbrellas dripping after their dash through the sideways, heavy rainfall, it only seemed natural to linger upon this interesting development while their garments and accessories dried a bit. Thus, they milled about near the cloak room, located by the front entrance.

Mr. and Mrs. Herman fussed over both of their daughters' demands. "Yes," Mrs. Herman agreed, patting her daughter's hand, "my daughters must have a maid to themselves. The sooner, the better."

Miss Augusta turned pleading eyes upon her father.

"Father, do not forget to inform the clerk we shall need several bellhops to help with our umbrellas on the way to our villa, and a ride in a covered motor car, certainly not the mule pulling the cart with our trunks."

"I fear our trunks are far too heavy for that one little mule. I do hope they have another cart. We have many more trunks and hat boxes than the first load." Lifting her sharply pointed chin, Miss Isadora sniffed.

"We have the key to your villa right here, Mr. and Mrs. Herman." The clerk held up the key. "We don't have many motor cars on Green Island, but I do have a bellhop or two we can spare." He pointed out the door. "If you follow along under the portico, it is but a short walk to the villas. The bellhops can escort you and see to it you are settled in."

"What is that divine smell?" Miss Augusta gave a dainty sniff. "I wish to breakfast before we settle into our villa, Father. Don't you?"

"I would like to visit the powder room." Miss Isadora talked partly over her sister. "I am the elder. You shall have to wait your turn about breakfast, Augusta."

"I shall do no such thing, but I do think we should inspect a menu. What if this particular dining room is not where the high society mingles for breakfast? How can we be certain?" Miss Augusta glanced nervously at the breakfast dining room.

"We'll want a view of the lake from our table." Mrs. Herman fussed with the ostentatious hat on her head before the clerk had a chance to inform them everyone ate in both dining rooms, but only the breakfast one in the morning unless guests chose to go out to a restaurant or order a meal in their accommodations.

"One moment, Mr. Herman." The clerk handed the villa key to Mr. Herman and snapped his fingers, calling a bellhop to his desk. "Warren. There you are. Please, find us four current breakfast menus, and do be quick about it."

"Yes, sir." Warren hastened away while several resort employees struggled with the heavy load on the cart outside the main entrance, rearranging items and attempting to cover the trunks with a tarp to protect them from the rain. They stacked some items temporarily on the covered porch. Abby could count at least twenty hat boxes. She felt sorry for the mule and the elderly driver, both being pelted by rain while waiting for the family to reappear with a villa key. The Hermans gave them no consideration as Warren returned with the menus and the family began studying them.

The front door opened, and a gust of wind blew in as Abby slid her umbrella into a bronze holder with those of her family's. The earl and the tycoon's son sauntered into the foyer, heading toward the dining room. The maître d' fussed over them, drawing Miss Augusta's attention.

The debutante narrowed her eyes and whispered.

"Did you hear, Mother? One gentleman had a British accent, and the waiter called him Lord-something-or-other. I think he's a duke. Let us go at once to the dining room. If it's good enough for him, it is good enough for us."

Augusta tossed her menu onto the front desk and drew her mother to the breakfast dining room entrance, abandoning all previous demands. Isadora stomped a foot and picked up the front of her ruffled skirt, following with a sigh. Mr. Herman trailed his family—poor man. The clerk shook his head in exasperation and gathered up the menus, hurrying to give the cart driver a master key to the Herman villa.

In the meantime, the maître d' returned from seating the earl. Miss Augusta insisted upon a table assignment for four as close to the lord's table as possible. Mr. Herman opened his wallet as his daughter grew impatient while the host considered the matter, doling out a generous tip to accomplish the request.

Grandmother nudged her cane toward where the Herman family had stood in line. "There goeth a tempest in a teapot."

"Pardon?" Catherine frowned.

Abby translated as Gran led them toward the dining room. "Katie-bug, what Grandmother meant is to keep a safe distance."

Elizabeth shook her head. "I'm surprised the steamship didn't sink from the weight of those feathers and ruffles. Did you see the size of Mrs. Herman's hat?"

"How could we miss it?" Catherine choked out. "'Tis the size of Florida."

Gran leaned toward them. "Some feel they must flaunt their finery, but the truly rich in Christ have no need. Chin up, girls. 'Let your light so shine that men may see your good works,' not your frippery."

CHAPTER 11

It appears that God has deliberately left us in a quandary about many things... He did not spare us. He wants us to reach maturity. He has so arranged things that if we are to go on beyond the "milk diet" we shall be forced to think.

— ELISABETH ELLIOT

The next morning at breakfast, the rain stopped long enough for Ryan to appear with Jack and asked if they would care to proceed with Elizabeth's photography session. Elizabeth nearly choked down the last few bites of her oatmeal. Abby and Catherine finished their fried eggs, and giving Gran a kiss on the cheek, they left her to enjoy a book club meeting with Ava and Blanche. At the villa, Elizabeth changed into a white blouse and black skirt to match the garments Ryan's grandmother wore in the portrait. Then Jack and Ryan escorted them to Ryan's yacht.

"It has more space than my rowing boat. Welcome aboard, everyone." Ryan pointed out seating and in no time at all, he pushed a button and the engine fired up.

Ryan steered them across Lake George in grand style to the Grand Forks dock where a carriage and driver waited. Once they'd transferred to the carriage, the driver navigated a handsome team of chestnut horses to the hotel which also served as the Steele family lodgings. Elizabeth looked as if she had climbed Mount Everest. Abby could hardly wait to see the hotel, but Ryan warned them it didn't have the amenities of Sagamore.

"We only offer horseback riding, boating, hiking trails, comfortable lodgings, and delicious food, but the natural beauty and easy, quiet pace seems attractive to many patrons," Ryan explained. "There is a small village nearby to explore, as well."

"Nothing wrong with that," Jack said.

"Ideal for writers," Abby added.

"I'm sure it's very pleasant," Elizabeth responded.

Once inside the two-story, modest establishment with a cluster of cottages nearby for those who desired larger accommodations than a hotel room, Ryan introduced them to his parents and the photographer, Mr. Jameson, arriving shortly after they did.

"'Tis nice to finally meet you all, and of course, to see you again, Jackson. It's been a few years. You have grown since then." Mrs. Steele smiled at Jack from behind the front desk and studied Elizabeth, Abby, and Catherine with a warm but apprehensive look.

Mr. Steele, more relaxed as he nodded at his wife's words, reached across the counter and shook hands with Jack. "Jack, it's good to see you." Facing Elizabeth, he added, "Goodness, you do look like my Alice's great-grandmother."

They turned to glance at the portrait above the fireplace in the spacious reception room, but before they could take it in, Ryan's mother said, "Here is the shawl. We've kept it in a trunk over the years. I don't know how it's lasted so long, but her wedding dress used to be with it. My mother was married in it, but it became worn, and I couldn't wear it for our wedding. In any case, the velvet shawl survived." She handed Elizabeth an elegant, tasseled coral shawl which clearly matched the one in the painting.

"Thank you, Mrs. Steele." Elizabeth ran her hands over the fabric and sighed, in awe of the accessory. "It's beautifully preserved."

Mrs. Steele nodded. "My grandmother and mother would be proud of this moment."

Abby and Catherine followed Elizabeth as she inspected the reception room, complimenting Ryan and his family on the combination of rustic decor and elegant cherry furniture, much as the Sagamore and other homes and resorts in the Adirondacks did.

Pleasant groupings of sofas, chairs, and tea tables in both styles dotted the spacious room.

"I do like the charm of this lovely room with the wood floors and the contrasting stone fireplace." Elizabeth shared her praise with Ryan while his parents looked on from behind the front desk. "And your cottage is not far from here, correct, Ryan? Pity we won't have time to see it today."

"That's right. I live in my place here on the property, but my parents have a pleasant suite upstairs," Ryan explained. "They like to be close to the front desk for our patrons."

The photographer positioned a wooden stool near one side of the fireplace beneath the portrait. Abby joined Catherine and Elizabeth to study the painting of Ryan's ancestor, taking in the striking resemblance to their cousin.

"Goodness, the two of you could almost be twins," Abby breathed.

Catherine nodded. "Remarkable."

Jack reached Abby's side, poised with a notebook and pencil. He grinned. "In case I need to jot anything down for my article."

Elizabeth's confidence kicked in and she draped the shawl across one shoulder, leaving the other end to rest low on her other arm, like the positioning of the shawl in the portrait. She sat down on the stool where the photographer indicated.

Ryan stood out of the way with Jack while the

photographer fussed with rearranging the drapes to enable the most light to stream inside.

"How do I look?" Elizabeth directed her question to Abby and Catherine, sitting up tall and straight on the stool.

"Just about right," Abby said.

"Stunning," Catherine agreed. "Remember not to smile too much."

Elizabeth pressed her lips together and smoothed her brow, sitting up even straighter and tilting her head. "Is this stoic enough?"

Abby and Catherine burst into giggles, nodding. Elizabeth couldn't help but laugh. Then she recovered her composure and another serious expression. Catherine stepped forward to arrange the shawl to suit the portrait one more time since Elizabeth's giggles had displaced it. "There," she said, backing away.

"Lift your chin half an inch and turn your face to the right about one inch," Abby directed. "That's it. You've got it."

"Hold the pose right there." The photographer stepped forward, ready to do his work. He took several pictures from various angles, his contraption making lots of noise and bulb flashes with each snap. "You're a natural at this, Miss ...?"

"Parker. Elizabeth Parker," Elizabeth answered proudly. "I do hope this helps Grand Forks restore her days of glory."

"Excellent," the photographer said. "This will fascinate the locals and draw many more folks here. The lodge has quite a history. One of the first in the area, all started by the lady in the portrait and her husband, many years ago. You and Ryan make a lovely couple too."

Elizabeth blushed. What could she say to the remark? She hadn't known Ryan long enough for their relationship to progress beyond an informal summer courtship. When they returned to Ohio, would Ryan write to her? Would something more come of their relationship? Of Abby's with Jack? Only time would tell. But judging by Ryan's relaxed posture and expression as he leaned against a column, he didn't put any great stock by the comment. Abby could only hope she had misinterpreted something about their relationship, but today more than ever, she sensed Ryan's casual disinterest in his efforts to court Elizabeth in contrast with her cousin's enthusiasm about all things Ryan. Thus far, the day's event seemed to emphasize Ryan Steele's intent to profit from Elizabeth's good looks and resemblance to his ancestor rather than to enhance and deepen their friendship into something more. Abby couldn't put her finger on it, but if she had to guess, she would think Ryan floundered somewhere between distraction with business matters and a struggle to hold it all together around his friends. Competing with the Sagamore couldn't be easy.

"How old would you say your great-grandmother was when the portrait was made?" Jack inquired.

Ryan straightened. "About the age of twenty. My great-grandfather commissioned the portrait a year after they married."

"I am nineteen. Nearly the same age," Elizabeth marveled, looking up at the portrait.

"And they had how many children?" Jack scratched down the information.

"One son and a daughter, like my parents had Cora and me. My sister was sorry she couldn't be here today. She had something to do in Bolton with a friend." Ryan reached into his suit jacket pocket and produced an envelope. "Ma made some notes for your article. Their names and other details are written down."

Jack opened the envelope and glanced over the notes. "This is helpful. Thank you. It will be a much better article than I had previously hoped. I began thinking about how little I know about the history of Grand Forks. I only know it's been here as long as I've known you and your family, Ryan."

"We're all done with the pictures, Mr. Steele." The photographer shook Ryan's hand as Elizabeth slid off the stool and returned the shawl to his mother. "I'll drop by when the photographs are ready. You'll need to choose one for the article Jackson is writing. Of course, my editor said we'll run it in the *Bolton Gazette*."

"Thank you, Mr. Jameson." Ryan smiled. Jack shook hands with the photographer, too, and then the man hurried away, likely anxious to go to his next appointment. Ryan turned to Elizabeth. "Thank you for doing this, Elizabeth."

"Of course." She dipped her head in acknowledgement. "Maybe you could have a mannequin wearing the same wardrobe and shawl positioned near the photograph once it's framed—you know, to bring the history to life and display the shawl. It's so thick and well-preserved, I think you'd only have to worry about fading. Perhaps keeping it as far from the windows as possible would help."

Mrs. Steele smiled, looking at her husband. "I like Elizabeth's idea. Our customers would enjoy it. I think we could arrange something, don't you, Philip?"

He nodded. "I do. I'll see if I can order one of those mannequins."

"Do come by sometime for dinner with us," Mrs. Steele said to everyone. Then she yawned. "Dear me. I've not been sleeping so well these days. It's time for a lie-down. I hope you don't mind if I excuse myself. I've been looking forward to this moment, but now I have worn myself out in the excitement."

"It's no trouble at all, and a pleasure meeting you. I'm sure we can catch up at dinner sometime, perhaps to look at the photos and choose one for the newspaper," Elizabeth remarked, her pretty blue eyes brightening.

Abby could tell her cousin longed for a chance to spend time with Ryan, but she wondered how Elizabeth could succeed in getting him to open up to her more.

On the carriage ride returning to the yacht, Ryan made an effort to carry on small talk with her, asking about her dance lessons and badminton, but questions plagued Abby. For one thing, they hadn't seen a single customer in the hotel during the visit. Did their business flounder more than he let on? For another, Ryan did not pay nearly enough attention to Elizabeth, in her opinion. Troubled, she worried her cousin would end up with a broken heart if Ryan did not step up a good deal more or make his intentions clear if he intended to do otherwise. Yet another quandary to consider and she could do little about a remedy except pray.

CHAPTER 12

We must be willing to let go of the life we have planned, so as to have the life that is waiting for us.

— E.M. FORSTER

*A*bby accomplished a great deal of writing during the next few days when rainy weather returned, as if it had only paused long enough to afford Elizabeth her debut as a model for Ryan's family. Bolts of thunder and lightning flashed in the sky and kept everyone on their toes, but occasionally, the rain subsided into a drizzle before working into a frenzy again. She didn't see Jack on rainy days. Perhaps he huddled in his villa, writing, ordering room service. But she found herself watching for him around every corner.

When the sunshine reappeared after breakfast three days later, Abby went walking with the intention of spending time reading outdoors. Stuck on a chapter in her own manuscript agonizing her about how to proceed, she tucked an Emily Dickinson poetry book under her arm with a quilt and headed toward a meadow on the north side of the stables. She spread the blanket, then settled on her tummy, the book in her hand, ankles crossed and heels pointed upward. With stockings, a petticoat, and her long skirt billowing around her shins, she needn't worry about showing any skin.

She hadn't been there long when horse hooves approached from behind, causing her to look up and catch her breath, then chuckle. Jack rode toward her on a stallion. The rain had cooled the island considerably, and he'd donned his Sherlock disguise again.

"Good morning, Jack. Sweltering yet in that get-up?" Abby held her straw hat to her head as she smirked up at him, the brim doing a nice job of keeping the sunshine from her eyes.

Jack dismounted and tied the stallion to a tree trunk. "You're a sight for sore eyes, looking pretty as a rose in a garden."

"Thank you." Abby smiled, her heart squeezing. "Don't ask how my writing is going since I'm stuck, but how's yours?"

"It's going well." He sat down on the quilt. "I've

started the mystery and finished some articles which may be fit for publication after some thorough rounds of editing, including Ryan's article." He sat cross-legged on the quilt and tossed his cloak within reach, withdrawing a pair of binoculars from a pocket. He held up the binoculars and peered through them to the southwest.

"Are you admiring the view or investigating a crime?"

"I never know what I will find on these nature rides. Stunning scenery, for starters." Jack held the binoculars steady.

"May I have a look?" She set the book aside and sat up, swinging her ankles together to her right. Then she smoothed her gown, ensuring she covered her ankles properly, chiding herself for not doing so when he arrived. He handed her the binoculars. She held them over her eyes and looked toward the southern side of Green Island. "I don't see anything except gorgeous pine, maple, and oak trees, but Lake George fairly shimmers today."

"If you look over this way, you can see the rear of the main house, the villas, and the stable." Keeping the binoculars pressed to her eyes, he directed her view to the rear of the Sagamore's main house and the dirt road leading to it. Abby blinked. They'd crossed that road on horseback.

"What am I looking for? All I see is a dirt road and

...” Her voice trailed away. “Oh, I see a figure. Walking. Hmm. I think it's Mr. Rhodes. Why, yes, it is Mr. Rhodes. He was following along the road, but good grief!” Abby's mouth fell open. “He just laid down on the side of the road, in the dirt. No, he's sitting up again, adjusting his suit coat, smashing his hat a bit. Now he's lying down again, quite deliberately, leaving his hat on his chest. No, he's sitting up and ripping his suit. Of all the crazy things I've ever seen! Now he's lying down again in the road.”

“What? Let me see!” Jack breathed, swiping the binoculars. “By George, you're right! He is lying on the side of the road. How odd.”

“Why do you suppose he's doing all of this? Clearly, it's a ruse.” Abby frowned.

“Frankly, I have no idea, Miss Watson.” Jack kept the binoculars focused on the manager. “He's certainly up to something, or else he's lost his mind.”

“I wonder how long he intends to lay there.” Abby faced Jack. “Did you ever speak with Ryan about the salt incident?”

Jack studied Mr. Rhodes through the binoculars while he spoke. “Yes, I did, when I gave him the article. Ryan said he was fine. We would have had lunch, but it was raining, I'd already eaten, and they'd delivered the wrong food. I'd ordered a steak, and they brought me a chef salad. Men don't like rabbit food when they want steak. I asked if he'd heard about the salty tomato bisque incident. He said yes, he'd heard about it when he went to use the pump to rinse off his new boots and encountered Marguerite, one of the kitchen maids, talking with Abel, the assistant chef."

"I see. What did he say about the conversation?" Abby straightened, her eyes widening.

"Marguerite had made the statement, 'it served him right.' Ryan asked what she'd meant." Jack looked up from the binoculars at Abby. "She said she'd let Abel tell the story since it was his to tell. Abel explained he spiked the soup with too much salt because the head chef, Oscar, is rude. He wanted to get Oscar into trouble. Ryan promised not to tell anyone and swore me to secrecy. Anyhow, that night—I assume before we saw him at dinner—Ryan said he went inside the kitchen after this discussion with Marguerite and Abel to say hello to the staff as he often does, but while there, he stepped in an enormous pile of salt Abel had spilled from his shenanigan. Hence, the grains of salt in the tracks, which I did not admit to knowing. Then he washed his boots a second time. He thought it a good joke on Oscar, but he agreed, not so good for business or his new boots. I think we can rule out Ryan from having anything to do with the salt incident, but I'm not sure about the other events. I didn't bring those up, of course."

"I see." Abby twisted her lips to one side. "It seems now we have a good idea the soup incident was separate from the others. Maybe that's all the Lord wanted us to conclude, perhaps to guide us into considering who else could be involved in the saddle and ransacking incidents."

He nodded, raising the binoculars again. "I agree, but it appears the Texan and the Englishman on a horseback ride have discovered Mr. Rhodes. Rhodes is pretending to be passed out, and they're about to rescue him. Help him back to the resort, I presume."

"Why do you suppose Rhodes would do such a thing?" she asked, shaking her head.

"I'm not sure, but I have my suspicions." He set the binoculars aside and turned to her, pulling her hands into his. "Miss Greenwood, may I escort you to the dance on Friday?"

Abby smiled. She'd nearly forgotten about the dance until Catherine had informed her Edwin had asked if he could escort her. "Yes, Sherlock, you may, but no costume, right?"

"I guess this means the fancy duds," he said, causing her to laugh. Then he removed his fake mustache and leaned forward. "May I kiss you, Abigail?"

She nodded, afraid to disturb the moment with words, allowing him to brush her cheek with a sweet and tender kiss, then barely brushing her lips with his before he pulled away. Opening her eyes after the sweet moment, Abby saw green leaves and blue sky spinning about in a beautiful reverie, making her smile. She laughed as he put the mustache on again. Jack certainly could make her laugh, possessing a playful way about him which she loved.

"Would you mind telling me your favorite flowers?"

"Jack, you don't have to bring me flowers."

"I want to. Maybe a wrist corsage."

"I love all flowers, but especially blue bachelor buttons, sweet pea, zinnias, and hydrangea. Roses are nice too." She smiled, toying with a button on her sleeve. "I'll be wearing a gown in a shade of periwinkle. No red or orange flowers for this particular gown, and the right blue might be complicated."

"So pink, white, purple, violet, lavender. Got it." Jack stood, returning the binoculars to his pocket inside the cloak. "I'd best go. I need to find out what Rhodes is up to. I have a sinking feeling it's not good. I think the earl and his cousin have taken him to the resort."

She nodded. "See you tomorrow. And Jack, I won't be at dinner tonight. Catherine is making a stew and homemade buttermilk biscuits in our kitchenette for her beau, and I'm to go with Elizabeth to dinner with Ryan to help choose a photograph for the newspaper article."

"Ah, yes. I gave it to Ryan when I spoke to him. It's kind of a conflict of interest for me, but I'll explain later." He glanced at his pocket watch and then mounted his horse.

"See you around." She waved. "Do tell me what you learn about Rhodes."

He tipped the brim of his hat. "Will do, ma'am." Jack urged the horse into a trot.

For a while, Abby sat there on the quilt enjoying the peaceful moment, reveling in the lingering smell of his musky sandalwood cologne. No need to let Rhodes disturb her luxurious reading time. Jack left her in quandary enough.

CHAPTER 13

Then shall the virgin rejoice in the dance, both young men and old together: for I will turn their mourning into joy, and will comfort them, and make them rejoice from their sorrow.

— JEREMIAH 31:33

"Jack, I heard Mr. Rhodes told the police someone attacked and robbed him of the bank deposit for the Sagamore. You and I both know the truth. What should we do?" Abby asked as he whirled her around Sagamore's ballroom the next evening.

He'd brought her a wrist corsage of sweet pea blooms in shades of pink, purple, and white. The corsage looked lovely over her evening-length white gloves, and the gown she wore fit exquisitely, featuring folds of the soft fabric draping above her slim waist, the skirt gathered into more folds leading to a demi-train.

"It's all right. I've told the police what we saw. They may want to speak with you for confirmation, but not tonight." Jack kept his voice low as he held her arm above her head and turned her in a graceful twirl. "Tonight belongs to us."

But she couldn't quite put the mystery from her mind. "Jack, could the Sagamore be liable for the horseback riding injuries Lena suffered?" Her brows furrowed. "I don't think the Carters plan to pursue a case, but could the resort be held responsible for negligence if anything else happens to their guests?"

"Now you sound like my father." Jack chuckled as she settled closer to his shoulder after the twirl. "It's possible, but a judge's decision could also find in the resort's favor, depending on how the case is argued. In Brumfield v. McIntosh, a Kentucky case from 1889, a judge ruled in favor of the horse's owner when a visitor to a horse farm brought action for negligence after sustaining an injury by the owner's mare. The judge ruled the owner had no duty to prevent the mare from falling against the fence, nor a duty to warn visitors of the possibility of such an accident to occur."

"Oh, I see. Not that I don't feel for injured parties because I do, but I've grown rather fond of the place. I'd hate to see them put out of business." Abby sighed when the waltz came to an end and Jack returned her to their seats near Grandmother. They settled into the comfortable chairs and sipped punch from the glasses he'd brought them earlier.

Jack leaned closer, looking attractive in his black tuxedo and bow tie. "Now you begin to understand why my father sent me to law school. I wouldn't want to make it common knowledge, but he's one of several investors in the Sagamore, not to mention other investments and business ventures. As I said before, my task is to protect the family assets."

"I see what you meant about writing the article for Grand Forks being a conflict of interest in a way. I'm glad you decided to help your friend and his family with their hotel. They don't have the amenities or scale of the Sagamore." She paused, thinking about Jack's task. "Your law degree will certainly help you with the events happening around here. I'm sure your father has great confidence in you. What do you think will become of Mr. Rhodes?" she whispered.

"I don't know yet. We need more proof of what he's been up to, but we know he's not to be trusted."

Abby nodded. "Have you spoken to your father about yesterday's strange behavior? Clearly, he tried to make it look like a robbery when it was not the case."

"I telephoned my father yesterday evening. I'm not sure what the board will decide to do, but some decision will be made soon," Jack assured her in a low voice so Grandmother wouldn't hear their discussion. "Rhodes is kind of like the wallpaper. He's worked here since I can remember. It's a difficult situation for them. They've always liked his work."

For a while, she pondered his answer, contenting herself to observe Katie-bug dancing with Edwin. Catherine finally looked truly happy. Elizabeth danced with Ryan on the other side of the floor. The sinfonia had returned to make the evening special, their seats taking up a large corner platform of the ballroom. She turned to speak to her grandmother, who seemed a million miles away, lost in her own thoughts. "Doesn't Catherine look cute dancing with Edwin, Grandmother?"

"Pardon? Oh, Edwin and Catherine. Yes, indeed. It's the other fellow dancing with Elizabeth—that Ryan—who I don't trust," Gran replied, holding tight to her cane.

Abby glanced at Jack. Had he heard the remark? Yes, judging from the way he studied Fanny Wiltshire. She pressed her lips together, then attempted to explain as gently as possible. "Grandmother usually has a keen sense of intuition about the character of others. She's seldom far from the mark."

"I can't put my finger on it, but there's just something not right about the boy." Grandmother's eyes narrowed as she continued to watch Ryan dancing with her granddaughter.

"He's not really a boy at his age, Gran. How old are you, Jack? Twenty-seven? Isn't Ryan about the same age?" Abby asked.

"I'm twenty-eight and he is twenty-six," Ryan answered.

"Age has little bearing on one's character," Grandmother reminded Abby.

"I can't argue with that." But she could change the subject. "I am having a chuckle that Miss Augusta and Miss Isadora are smoldering about the earl asking no ladies to dance."

"I think they'd frighten even the most desperate of souls away," Gran commented with a glance toward where the architect and his family occupied a row of seats against the opposite wall of the ballroom. "No amount of wealth is worth spending one's future in the company of those who will inflict suffering, pain, and demands for the rest of eternity."

Jack began to laugh, but before either he or Abby could reply, Grandmother's friend Ava approached in a dazzling ballgown and took the seat between them. "Hello, Jackson and Abigail." Then she turned to Gran. "Have you heard the news, Fanny?"

"What news?" A curious expression crossed Gran's face.

"A group of young boys of about the ages of sixteen and seventeen went on the mainland hiking with the Sagamore's Indian guide yesterday and never returned.

They were expected back last night around ten or eleven o'clock."

"Oh, my! No wonder so many young ladies of my granddaughters' age aren't dancing. I thought it seemed like some of the boys were missing." Grandmother sighed. "What is to be done? I thought the Sagamore's guide is reputed to be one of the best. He's a local, from what I understand."

"Yes, he is, but Mr. Rhodes—after he was beaten and robbed yesterday afternoon by some island thief —has placed one of his assistants in charge, Beau Destin. Beau has been reluctant to send anyone looking for the boys because the guide is reportedly among the finest, but now he's forming a search party. They are to leave after the dance, as I understand it. Of course, the parents are extremely concerned and are demanding some course of action be taken," Ava explained.

"What a dreadful situation," Grandmother replied, Abby and Jack nodding along but unable to share what they knew about Mr. Rhodes. "How many boys are missing?"

"Well, let's see." Ava held up a gloved hand and began counting on her fingers. "Samuel Reed, the New York banker's son; Harvey and Jacob Crandall, the English writer's sons; Hugh and Charlie Brantley, two of the clockmaker's four sons; Homer Gardmont, the son of our ambassador to France; and Alexander Lloyd, the other banker's son. Seven boys, all missing."

Abby turned to Jack. "Will you become part of the search party if you are asked, Jack?"

"I imagine so."

Abby's heart skipped a beat. "Do be careful."

"I will. I've hiked through the area beyond the island on a few other occasions. Don't worry overmuch." Jack tilted his head toward her and gave her a stern look.

She bit her lip. Too late. The worry had begun as soon as she'd heard the words, search party. "I promise, I'll try not to worry. We'll pray everyone returns safely."

"Yes, we will definitely be praying," Grandmother added. "The ambassador and his wife and daughters must be frantic. No wonder they aren't here this evening. I'll be sure to send a note of comfort to Ellen."

Abby glanced toward the couples dancing again. "It's a good thing Edwin wasn't among them, or Catherine would be sobbing her heart out in her room. I'm surprised he and his younger brother—James, I believe—didn't go with the other boys."

"Oh, goodness. A sobbing granddaughter would be the very last thing I need on my hands." Grandmother rolled her eyes. "I wonder why he and his brother didn't go with the others."

Abby shrugged. "I don't know, but I'm awfully glad he didn't. Maybe their parents wisely said they could not go traipsing about in the wilds."

Jack leaned closer. "Would you care for a stroll on the balcony, Abby?"

"I'd love to," she replied. "Is it all right with you, Gran? We won't be gone too long."

Grandmother glanced at Abby and waved her on. "I'll be fine."

Abby smiled and Jack pulled her to her feet. They hurried away, ducking through a set of French doors onto the balcony running along the length of the ballroom.

"Look how beautiful Lake George looks this evening in the moonlight," Abby said when they paused near the railing to admire the way the moon cast a shimmering swath of golden light across the ripples of water.

"It's breathtaking, but not nearly as beautiful as you are, Miss Abigail Greenwood." Jack's voice grew low and husky as he pulled her into his arms. "May I kiss you before I leave with the search party?"

She nodded, overcome with shyness at being in his arms, alone on the balcony with such a handsome gentleman.

He gave her another kiss, his mouth warm and tender on her lips.

"Oh, Jack ..." Abby melted in his embrace, her knees quivering as he tucked the cascade of her brown curls over her shoulder.

For a little while, he held her there, the two of them admiring the view and enjoying the smell of honeysuckle wafting from the blooms below. Then he interrupted the silence. "How is your writing coming along? You said you were stuck."

She laughed, nodding. "Why, yes, I am."

"What seems to be the problem?"

"I've come to the portion of my memoir where I need to write about a miracle that may seem quite unbelievable to the reader."

"Why is that?"

Abby sighed. "Okay, I'll try to explain, but it's hard. I mean, this miracle isn't like the others. It stands out, and I don't wish to draw criticism from the naysayers. A man who was missing an arm came to the Azusa Street Mission and went forward for prayer. Struggling to find work, he was doing his best under the circumstances. The evangelist prayed for him, and the Lord supernaturally re-grew his arm right before our eyes. First, the bone appeared, then the sinews, veins, muscles, and then skin. It was the most amazing and memorable miracle I've ever witnessed. The power of God was on display like never before. Jack, I don't even know how to do it justice in my writing, nor do I know if readers will believe me."

He rested his hands on her shoulders and turned her to face him. "Abby, for what it's worth, I believe you. Secondly, just write it the best you can. Believe in yourself and the gift you have within to write. How the reader responds and whether they believe is not your problem. That's their problem. The critics and naysayers are not your problem either."

She dropped her chin, internalizing the truth he spoke.

"It seems to me, all God is asking you to do is share what you saw from your perspective. It is your story, and no one can take that away from you. God worked the miracle. You witnessed it. Others there saw it too. And it's the reader's problem if they walk away skeptical. If you do your part to the best of your ability, that's all God is asking."

Abby smiled up at him. "Jack, you don't know how much I needed to hear those words. I hate the idea I could be drawing a critic into the ring, but you're right. It's their problem, not mine."

He grinned. "And now we should return to the dance, or your grandmother will not consider me right about anything ever again."

She nodded and reached for his hand, pulling him inside. "True. She can be—shall we say—protective? Anyhow, I want to dance and dance."

Her lighthearted words covered the simmering emotions within. Who could have guessed that this man she'd thought haughty, rakish, ungentlemanlike, and shallow would encourage her in so many ways?

But a nagging in the back of Abby's mind reminded her she could not allow herself to fall in love with Jackson Gable, no matter how much she enjoyed his kisses, attention, fine dancing, and flirtations. Hadn't he said he wanted to take his time finding his queen? She really must protect her heart, and didn't she intend to enjoy her independence and establish herself as a writer? Summer would come to an end sooner rather than later. Would she end up with a broken heart when they parted?

No ... she should enjoy his affection but hold it loosely. Surely, he did not take her seriously. Doubts flooded her mind. The romance would turn out like any other summer fling of youth, and she should expect nothing more.

CHAPTER 14

Be careful for nothing; but in everything by prayer
and supplication with thanksgiving let your requests
be made known unto God.

— PHILIPPIANS 4:6

*A*bby finished writing about the magical prior
evening in her journal, then tucked the book
filled with her daily thoughts and favorite Scriptures
into a drawer in her desk. Had Jack and Ryan joined the
search party after the ball? The Adirondacks—fraught
with the dangers of thick forests, narrow passes, wild
animals, and places where civilization did not exist—
could hide a whole group of men. *Dear Lord, please bring
them home safely.* Hopefully, the moment her family
entered the main foyer, they'd hear the search party
had returned.

Time for breakfast. Satisfied with her blue-and-white-striped summer dress and the hat with the blue bow trailing over the brim she pinned on, Abby hurried downstairs to join her family for the walk to the main house.

But breakfast did not bring the news they'd hoped for. And the still-unknown whereabouts of the hiking group cast a bleak shadow upon the Sagamore's preparations for the Independence Day celebration in three days. While the kitchen made heaps of fried chicken and potato salad for a grand picnic and the assistant managers organized a fireworks display, worried mothers gathered in the island's chapel to pray for the return of their boys and the men who'd gone in search of them.

"Girls, I think we should join the mothers in prayer at the chapel," Grandmother suggested as they ate their breakfast in the unusually quiet dining room.

"Yes, Grandmama," Catherine agreed as Elizabeth and Abby nodded silently over their plates of pancakes, maple syrup, scrambled eggs, and bacon slices. They could hardly muster an appetite. Not given the absence of Jack, Ryan, and the seven missing boys. Neither did the earl, his cousin, or many of the other men appear. Abby would gladly kneel in prayer if it meant the safe return of their loved ones, friends, and companions.

At the altar in the chapel, Abby found a place to kneel, acknowledging the fear striking a chord of dissonance in her heart. In addition to her concerns for the missing boys, she wrestled with the real possibility of something happening to Jack. As much as she'd tried to prevent deep feelings for him from finding their way into her soul, she had to admit, the idea of never seeing him again troubled her. Only surrendering her fear of what the future might ultimately hold would give her courage and peace, but she could also implore the Lord to preserve and bring these men and boys home safely.

When Abby finished praying, she rose and found a seat on one of the wooden pews to wait for her family. Catherine took a seat beside her, but the arrival of Miss Augusta Herman with her sister and mother soon disrupted the quiet. The three walked in, their heels clicking and clacking on the stone floor. They reached the altar area, looking around with pinched expressions.

Augusta released a loud sigh. "I don't see an open spot to kneel." Did she not notice how even her loud whisper echoed throughout the small space?

"There's no room. Let's just sit on a pew." Isadora gestured behind them.

"No. Just squeeze in somewhere." Augusta elbowed her sister, and Isadora's silk skirts rustled as she tried to maintain her balance.

"Girls!" their mother hissed. "Stop acting like children. Must you always behave this way?"

Augusta made a disgruntled sound and rolled her eyes. Even if they were incapable of waiting quietly for someone to leave, didn't they see they could turn around and kneel at the front pew? They could make an altar at any pew. Perhaps they attended a church with strict rules of convention and were unaware that God only wanted people's hearts, not rigid rules and traditions.

Maybe they just needed someone to provide an example. She leaned over to Catherine and whispered, "I'm going to go help the Herman ladies find a place to pray."

Katie-bug's mouth dropped open. "I thought you said Grandmother wanted us to keep a safe distance."

"Yes, but I think the Lord also wants us to be friendly and kind when needed." Abby stood and slipped out of the aisle. Reaching Augusta, Abby smiled. She held out her arm toward the first pew and leaned near, whispering softly, "Ladies, if you'd like to kneel at the front pew, I will pray there with you since the altar is full. I'm sure the Lord will hear us from anywhere."

This resulted in the first smiles Abby had seen from the Herman ladies. They followed, kneeling at the front pew. Abby prayed again, beginning with a prayer of thanksgiving for the extra cushioning her garments provided. Perhaps the Lord would find humor in it, and since so many folks pestered Him for everything else, He might just need some humor and thankfulness. Then she prayed for the Herman family, Mr. Rhodes, and Ryan, asking Jesus to give them whatever each needed most. Then she prayed for the condition of her own heart and hidden attitudes she shouldn't harbor, such as judgmental thoughts, criticisms, unforgiveness, and anything else the Lord might want to show her.

While she knelt there in quietness before the Lord alongside Augusta, Isadora, and Mrs. Herman, Abby allowed a small smile. The Herman ladies had done her a world of good, after all. They'd given her a way to feel and show kindness toward them, both inwardly and outwardly, as well as opening an avenue to spend extra time in prayer herself. One could have wickedness in one's own heart and yet, blind to it, continue without repentance. The Holy Spirit was nudging her to continue to befriend the Herman family as Jesus had been a friend to her.

Please don't let me fall into blind wickedness, Lord. Preserve us all with the love and purity and righteousness You desire to cultivate in each of us. I will do my best to do as You have asked.

Feeling a sense of peace and release, Abby rose and joined Catherine, Elizabeth, and Grandmother, as the time to leave the chapel had come. While many of the mothers chose to linger, Abby followed her family outside. The Herman ladies trailed behind them.

"Miss Greenwood, is it not?" Augusta whisked around to Abby's side. "I just wanted to say, thank you. Thank you for praying with us and making room for us."

"Yes, of course, you're welcome," Abby replied, slowing her pace.

"We just wanted to do our part in this dreadful situation." Isadora, following closely behind, stepped in place beside them.

"Yes." Augusta bit her lower lip and then turned a hopeful glance toward Abby. "Would you and your family perhaps like to join us for tea later today? We are terribly bored and don't seem to have made any other friends since we've been on Green Island. I thought about going swimming, but with this disaster, it seems, well, perhaps a bit frivolous while lives hang in the balance."

"I understand. Well, um ..." Abby paused for Catherine, Elizabeth, and Grandmother to catch up. How would they feel about such an invitation, after Grandmother's warning?

Augusta laid a lace-gloved hand on Abby's arm. "It was kind of you to make room for us at the altar, Miss Greenwood, perhaps the kindest thing anyone has done for us in a long time."

Taken aback by Augusta's remarks, Abby recovered and made her decision. "We would be delighted to have tea sometime. There is also something you could do if you'd like to help. It may further the endeavor of making more friends while you are here."

Augusta gave a quick little nod, her eyes fastened on Abby's.

"For one, the mothers and siblings of the missing boys may need some comforting in the form of perhaps a basket of tea, scones, or cookies with a personal, handwritten note—if you like to bake and write little cards or letters. I'm sure it would be appreciated. I have some plans for today, but I could help tomorrow morning after the early church service."

"Oh, yes, I like these ideas very much," Augusta breathed, her green eyes brightening. Isadora nodded, and both golden-haired sisters looked pleased.

Mrs. Herman hesitated, then stepped forward with an approving smile. "Benevolence is a thoughtful way to reach hearts and make new friends."

"I would like to join you ladies tomorrow morning," Catherine added, drawing closer as well. "I like to bake, and I have a tea cookie and a scone recipe from our mother."

Elizabeth nodded. "We might need to go to the general store and purchase the supplies later today or first thing after church, but we could come to your villa around tnoon tomorrow."

"I am happy to write notes or make cards," Grandmother offered.

"Very good. We are in villa number five with a fully stocked kitchenette, including baking trays, mixing bowls, and utensils." Mrs. Herman's tone warmed as she spoke. "Perhaps we can get a few things baked today, and the rest tomorrow when you arrive. We'll have luncheon delivered too."

"We have plenty of paper, pens, lace, ribbon, and other items for making cards," Augusta added.

Abby smiled. "We'll see you tomorrow after church, then, ladies."

---

*W*hen they arrived at their own villa after the prayer vigil, Grandmother pulled the pins out of her hat and placed it on the foyer table. "Abigail, that was a splendid thing you did for the Herman ladies. You know how I detest when folks put on airs and so forth, but in this case, it seems they have decided to drop those pretenses which never work well when making friends under any circumstances."

"Thank you, Gran. I hope they are ready for our attempt at a genuine offer of friendship. I think they can see the others have not embraced the façade."

"Maybe they will learn something about the importance of discretion when it comes to speaking of the things God has bestowed upon us," Catherine added.

Abby raised a brow at her sister. "You never cease to amaze me, Katie-bug. Certain things come out of your mouth that convince me you are much older than seventeen inside that head of yours."

Catherine stuck her tongue out at Abby. Abby shook her head and sighed. Perhaps she'd spoken too soon.

The day progressed solemnly. They fasted the noonday meal as another appeal to move God's heart for the miracle everyone needed. Abby retreated to her room with a cup of tea and labored over the next scene Jack had encouraged her to write. Finally, she let out a small cry of victory as she yanked the last page out of the typewriter, trembling to hold it in her hands. Jack would smile if he could see the result of his encouraging words.

The mental war to battle with faith instead of fear returned at dinnertime as Abby and her family attempted to eat a meal together, but everyone's nerves seemed raw when there were so many empty seats in Sagamore's dining room. The mothers and siblings of the missing boys and wives of those who'd gone in search of them appeared weary. The Herman sisters waved and nodded from another table, and they returned the waves, but Grandmother did not invite anyone to sit with them that evening. Ava and Blanche did not appear, and the Carter ladies huddled together in a sorrowful state. It seemed to Abby, everyone needed space to steer away from conversation diluted with fear and worry.

Staring at her plate filled with cabbage casserole, sliced cucumbers, and Noodles Romanoff, Abby caught herself toying with the food, remembering her dances with Jack as she twirled her fork. She dropped the utensil and sighed. When would their boys return, her Jack among them?

"Would you like to try the brie and crackers appetizer, Abigail?" Grandmother leaned forward with a hopeful smile. "You've barely touched your food."

Abby made an uncertain sound.

Grandmother's thin lips firmed. "Don't sulk, girls. The good Lord will bring our boys home to Sagamore. In the meantime, we need to keep up our strength."

Abby offered a weak smile. "Sure. I'll try some brie and crackers."

Elizabeth slid the plate of green olives and pickled beets toward her. "You can have some of these too. I'm enjoying the Oysters Rockefeller, but I don't have room for appetizers *and* the black walnut cake. I didn't take as much exercise today. It seems pointless and vain to swim in the pool, play badminton, or take dance lessons when trouble looms, but I do hope our boys will return in time for the Fourth of July picnic and fireworks tomorrow."

"The cake is delicious," Catherine informed them after several bites, but then she listlessly laid down her fork. The dining room doors burst open and then it sounded as though someone knocked over a glass of liquid, spilling it onto a table. Gasps followed and all of this commotion near the door caused Abby to look up from her plate and then at Gran, their mouths dropping open. Did she dare to twist around in her seat with an expectation? Abby's heart leapt with hope.

The guests in the dining room began to clap and cheer until the room filled with thundering applause and whooping. She turned in her seat toward the main doors, and tears filled her eyes as the men of the search party streamed inside, followed by the missing teens and the guide. Boys greeted their mothers, family, and friends with arms open wide. Their clothing smudged with dirt and hair tousled, the young men nevertheless offered glowing smiles and cries of joy at the reunions.

Everyone rose to their feet, and the clapping continued for a moment. Standing, Abby caught sight of Jack and Ryan walking toward them, followed by the earl, Lord Monroe and his cousin, Tybalt Monroe, the cattle tycoon's son. Ryan stepped toward Elizabeth as Jack embraced Abby, lifting her feet off the ground and swinging her around in a bear hug she would not soon forget. Why did it feel so good to be in his arms?

"Jack!" she breathed.

After a few moments, he released her, smiling, his blue eyes more radiant than ever, then stood back with Ryan, the earl, and Tybalt. Clearly, they'd become friends on their mission. "Any room at this table for four hungry men? We need a bath and a shave, but if you can stand us, food is the first order of business."

"Of course, please, gentlemen, join us." Grandmother indicated the extra seats at their table with an outstretched arm. "You are heroes. It is we who would be honored."

No one seemed happier than the mothers in the room that evening, but a place in Abby's heart reawakened with Jack at her side.

CHAPTER 15

He has shown you, O mortal, what is good. And
what does the Lord require of you? To act justly and
to love mercy and to walk humbly with your God.

— MICAH 6:8, NIV

The fourth of July morning of baking and
writing notes proceeded as planned after
church—only now, more joyfully, for the newly
returned hikers and searchers and their families. The
Herman family and Abby's family lovingly prepared
each package, wrapping the baked goods in brown
paper, tying them with pink ribbon for women, blue for
men and boys. They chatted, laughed, and baked until
the Herman villa smelled of vanilla and nutmeg.
Catherine, Elizabeth, Augusta, and Isadora agreed they
would pass the packages out at the picnic. Abby could

only think of spending time with Jack. Mr. Herman occasionally appeared in the kitchen to taste their confections and later to join them in the dining room for a light lunch, looking pleased his daughters and wife had finally made some allies at Sagamore. They spent much of the afternoon speculating on the few details they'd heard about one of the boys becoming lost on the hike and how the guide had eventually found him. Abby could hardly wait to ask Jack more about the incident that had delayed the entire party. Thankfully, the Lord had ultimately protected them.

At the dinner-time picnic, everyone ate their fill of fried chicken, watermelon slices, and potato salad on the front lawn, seated on blankets and quilts. Afterward, families settled in to enjoy the remaining evening sunshine and sultry breeze from the lake in the hour or so remaining before the illuminations. A band played patriotic songs while families enjoyed ice cream and strolls about the perimeter, younger ones ran about waving red, white, and blue flags, and everyone enjoyed mingling. The joyous mood had everything to do with their men and boys safely returned to them.

Elizabeth sat beside Ryan on a quilt while Catherine and Edwin tossed firecrackers on a dirt patch at the edge of the clearing. The earl talked to Miss Jane Peterson about her father's wheat farm and Grand-mother about her hotels, her apple harvest, and the prime minister. Tybalt Monroe described his Texas ranch to Augusta. Thank goodness, Abby had convinced her to pay heed to the cattle tycoon's son and give up on the earl. She'd never seen anyone run away so fast as Lord Monroe had—in fact, he'd practically jumped over a young couple's toddler—when Augusta had tried to give him his care package earlier.

With all as it should be at Sagamore for the moment, Jack asked if Abby would enjoy a stroll.

"I would love to," she said, accepting his hand to help her rise.

They strolled along the perimeter of the wooded area hemming in the main house. "Abigail, you once said your grandmother took you somewhere different each summer. I have been meaning to ask about the other places she has taken you other than Los Angeles on the west coast, and now the Adirondacks on the east coast."

"I'm glad you asked. I'm including some mentions of my other summer memories in the memoir. When I turned thirteen, we visited Paris. The next summer, we set sail for London. Then Venice to ride in a gondola, on to Rome to tour the Sistine Chapel, and then Portugal for my fifteenth summer. We went to New York to stay in the Waldorf-Astoria. The next year, The Peabody in Memphis. We returned to Claridge's Hotel in London for my eighteenth summer and explored more of England, Scotland, and Ireland. Then the Omni Home-stead Resort in Hot Springs, Virginia, in the Allegheny Mountains. We stayed in the Hotel Alexandria in Los Angeles for my twentieth summer and spent a week in a beach cottage on the Pacific Ocean. This year, my twenty-first summer, we spent a week shopping in New York and enjoyed the new Knickerbocker Hotel before coming to Sagamore."

"And which summer did you enjoy most?"

Abby laughed. "It's hard to choose just one. I have loved each for something different. Grandmother spoils us rotten. I revel in the history and significance of the sites we visited, and I confess, I enjoyed the mountains. I loved London and Portugal, but the Sistine Chapel was a thrill. Walking through Montmartre in Paris and exploring Windsor Castle are also special memories. But I will always remember Azusa as the bedrock of my salvation and faith. When you see the power of God displayed like that, and fire raining down from heaven on the roof, but nothing is burning except the growing love and passion you have for the Lord after accepting Him into your heart, it's an unforgettable milestone. Peace floods the soul. It's magnificent."

Jack studied her face, nodding. "Yes, I remember when I decided to follow the Lord in water baptism. My grandmother and mother prayed for me during my rebellion beforehand."

"I can't imagine you as rebellious, except perhaps when I first met you. I deemed you a rake," she admitted, causing him to laugh.

He shrugged. "That could easily have become the case. My folks live in one of those country houses on the edge of Philadelphia. At thirteen, I was running with the wrong crowd. Rich kids from private school who didn't care. We broke into the local public school-house. Smashed the windows and made a mess of the place, but my conscience wouldn't let me rest."

Abby's steps slowed. "What happened?"

"Jesus came to me in a dream, calling me to return and repent, so I turned myself in. I experienced His mercy. The other boys, most of them older, faced charges, but the Lord spared me. I was never the same again after He offered me an escape. I had to do a lot of community service, but I made some new friends and seized my chance at a fresh start. Never regretted my decision to follow Christ."

Abby touched his arm. "Thank you for sharing that with me, Jack. You have a powerful story. I hope you write about it in your books. It seems the divine power of God has reached out to both of us. He saved, sancti-fied, and redeemed us, setting us apart for His service."

"Indeed." He nodded solemnly.

How amazing to be able to talk about these spiritual matters with a man. To be able to show him her deepest self. Abby's heart overflowed. "If I hadn't seen Azusa, I would have gone on acting out the traditions of Chris-tianity but not truly knowing Him. Maybe because my parents also prayed for me, Jesus found me in Azusa Street. I finally knew how much He loved me because He revealed His heart to me for myself and others. Minutes later, one of the believers in the meeting handed me the mission's newsletter and told me God wanted me to write for Him. I spent much of my time at Azusa helping them write the next newsletter."

Jack blew out a soft breath. "I wish it had been that easy for me to find my purpose. I stumbled into writing, maybe only because I love books and mysteries so much." He paused when some youths set off fire-crackers nearby on the paved walk under the portico. "My father insisted I go to law school, but when I was halfway through and he found out how much I loved journalism, he said he didn't care if I ever opened a law office or if I wrote hundreds of newspaper articles, so long as I took care of the corporate issues for his invest-ments. I said, all right, you've got a deal."

"I don't know how you did it." Abby shook her head. "That's a long time to go to school for something you don't really want to do."

"It wasn't so bad. I imagined the law cases I learned about as some part of the mysteries I would eventually write." Jack turned to study her. "Speaking of mysteries, have things been quiet around here while we were gone? Any other strange events?"

"All quiet at Sagamore, except I heard the one assistant manager, Beau Destin, telling the other assistant that Beau had been promoted to senior manager and someone had officially asked Mr. Rhodes to step down into an assistant's position."

"I see." Jack rubbed his chin. "I'm sure my father will explain more about the decision next time I speak with him."

She hadn't expected him to take the news so calmly. "You don't think they should press charges for theft? It seems they've gone rather light on him."

"I don't know what to think yet."

"I wonder if he had something to do with the other incidents," Abby said as they returned to the quilt.

"I do too." Jack helped her sit down, then joined her. "I keep thinking, at least no one has died with what's happened around here. It's nice to see the Carter family enjoying their holiday with their daughter recovered from the fall, especially since they return to Kentucky soon, and the boys are safely rescued."

Abby's lips parted. "Do you think this business with the boys had anything to do with these other things?" She hadn't considered the possibility.

"I don't think so. The party's return was delayed mainly because one of the boys was lost and another kept lagging behind because he couldn't keep up with everyone. Another sprained his ankle, and the guide didn't have anyone he could send to inform the resort until we met up with him, but by then, we were all anxious to stick together and fend off dangers as a group. None of these kids have been out in the wilderness this far from home, and he would have been responsible if something had happened to any of them. At one point, the guide tried to take a shortcut home, but the path was blocked and they all had to take the long way around. I know he could track a squirrel jumping through tree limbs, and he did find the young man who'd gotten lost before we reached him."

Abby listened to all he said, but when the band began to play again, she thought about his bravery for helping to bring the boys home, and the integrity he had gained as a young Christian learning through his mistakes, sacrificing for his family, and making it through a long haul to graduate from college. While they enjoyed the music, he took her hand in his and Abby felt a tug on the strings of her heart. The amount of warmth, comfort, and happiness at having him "home" at the Sagamore swelled in her soul, kind of like the kind of cozy goodness and safety she'd often felt when holding a cup of warm spiced cider, drawing close to a crackling fire on a cold winter evening, and observing Ma stir a pan of stew at the cookstove. Dusk fell and the anticipation of the firework show stirred the crowd. She almost wished Jack wasn't such an incredible man. She was running out of reasons not to fall in love with him.

CHAPTER 16

The light of the righteous rejoiceth: but the lamp of
the wicked shall be put out.

— PROVERBS 13:9

*T*he next few weeks at Sagamore progressed
in relative peace. However, one beautiful day
in mid-July, Grandmother insisted the girls attend afternoon tea on the VanDyne villa's terrace. To prepare for
the tea, Abby, Elizabeth, and Catherine picked black-
berries growing in the woods and baked blackberry
scones.

After Mrs. VanDyne and her daughters praised the
pastries and spoke about the weather and the
upcoming regatta, Grandmother inquired as to whether
Mrs. VanDyne had recovered her address book and
letters. That lady sighed, answering no.

Abby pondered the visit for days. Something nagged at her, but she couldn't put her finger on what. Meanwhile, Elizabeth pined for Ryan, having seen him sparingly since the Fourth of July picnic.

"There's something I don't like about Ryan Steele," Grandmother repeated as she leaned back on one of the chaise lounges on their own villa's terrace one lazy summer afternoon. "For one thing, we never see him at church, while Abby's Jack is often in attendance." At the comparison, Abby didn't dare move from her spot by the French doors. She held her breath as Gran continued. "Have you spoken to him about his faith yet?"

"Not much, but I intend to ask him more." Elizabeth defended her beau from a neighboring chaise. "He works hard to help his parents, but I wish he could carve out more time with me. He did say he would come fetch me to dress the mannequin, and our news article and my photograph comes out in print soon."

Gran grumbled, "I thought he would have hinted at a ring by now, especially after this portrait business."

"We only just met in June," Elizabeth protested a bit crossly. And that proved a good time for Abby to retreat upstairs to write.

Nonetheless, Ryan appeared the next day at breakfast, more attentive than usual to Elizabeth. He even brought her a bouquet of wildflowers. After, he took Elizabeth, Catherine, and Edwin to dress the mannequin, serving them lunch at Grand Forks. They didn't see him for another week until the evening after the newspaper article released. Abby carefully cut a clipping of the article and the stunning photograph so Elizabeth could preserve it in her memory book. They purchased extra copies to mail home to Abby's parents and her cousin's parents, Aunt Minnie and Uncle Harold. A steady stream of Sagamore's patrons complimented Elizabeth on her success at dinner. Ryan looked pleased when people spoke to him about Grand Forks, his great-grandmother, and the striking resemblance between her and Miss Parker.

Abby thought their relationship might improve at this juncture, until Ryan disappeared for a full week. Looking glum, he and Jack joined Abby, her family, and other friends in Sagamore's breakfast dining room.

"What's on your mind, Ryan?" Jack asked. "Reservations at Grand Forks are sure to be up soon. All of New York has seen the article by now. My editor ran it a few days ago."

"Someone has stolen the shawl from the mannequin at Grand Forks. We don't want the news to spread. We're hoping to find it or replace it with a replica," Ryan informed them.

Elizabeth's mouth fell open. "That's terrible news, Ryan."

After a waitress delivered their plates, Grandmother leaned over her French toast, her eyes wide. "What a shock! Another thief?" She reached for the tiny silver pitcher of syrup.

"But to steal a shawl? It makes no sense," Abby

mumbled as she sliced into her fried eggs. "I think I'm going to need more coffee."

Jack shook his head. "I'm sorry, Ryan. I do hope the shawl is recovered. I know it means a lot to your family and the legacy of Grand Forks."

"Thank you, everyone," Ryan said and stared into his coffee cup.

---

*L*ate the following morning, Abby waited with Jack in Sagamore's foyer for a picnic basket from the kitchen. They intended to spend an afternoon rowing along Millionaire's Row, admiring the homes and extraordinary views with a picnic lunch—if the order ever arrived.

While they were biding their time, Miss Augusta turned up because her tea tray hadn't arrived, nor had her maid. The clerk received her scolding. Apparently, the laundry house had also made a grave error by sending a Mrs. Crandall's petticoats and bloomers to the earl, who brought the items to the front desk and hurried away, flustered. Another fellow had ordered coffee and Belgian waffles with a side of broiled salmon, but his brunch hadn't arrived.

A waiter finally brought their picnic basket from the kitchen. Jack accepted it, and they fled from the disgruntled complaints. Mischief surely seemed afoot. The nagging feeling Abby had experienced during the visit with the VanDynes returned with a vengeance. It all had to do with the address book, and possibly the shawl. Someone still had Mrs. VanDyne's address book, but who? The police had failed to recover it.

Ryan had returned to the Sagamore to accompany Elizabeth on an outing that very morning. The sinking feeling in the pit of Abby's stomach caused her to suspect him, since all seemed calm in his absence. But perhaps Mr. Rhodes had more shenanigans up his sleeve, or it could be maybe someone else right under their noses. Since the thief would likely have Mrs. VanDyne's address book and letters in his or her possession, they simply had to investigate. She couldn't explain who'd taken the shawl, but maybe Jack could.

She broke his silence as he rowed their boat away from shore. "All right, Sherlock. We need to talk about what happened this morning."

"I suspect Mr. Rhodes more than ever."

Abby dangled one hand in the lake, letting the cool water run over her fingers. Disliking his answer, she shifted carefully in her seat and shook her head. "No, I think it's Ryan. He's back again, wreaking havoc." Cupping some of the water in her hand, she splashed him. "He's going horseback riding with Elizabeth today, and they intend to build a boat for the regatta afterwards."

He leaned away from the splash with a grin. Tucking the oars into the boat, he allowed his expression to grow pensive. "I don't think so, and I wish you'd stop saying you suspect him. He is my friend, after all. Mr. Rhodes has far more access to muck things up in his position. He could have changed the directions for deliveries to make Beau look badly in an attempt to regain his former position."

Abby's lips pinched together. "I can't understand why the owner of the Sagamore and board of investors decided to keep him on. We are eyewitnesses to his thievery."

"I spoke to my father, and he said despite one investor objecting to him remaining, the others felt he is a loyal, highly qualified but underpaid employee. They are aware he may have been skimming the cash registers for some time, but they see it as their fault for underpaying him. He also said they sympathize with his retirement predicament since it is the motive they believe caused him to steal."

"What is his retirement issue?" Abby tilted her head toward him and brushed a curl away from her eyes.

"Apparently, in reading through some prior annual employee reviews, Father found notes that Rhodes had complained on several occasions about his salary being too low for him to set aside an adequate amount for a timely retirement. He'd said he would be forced to reside with distant relations or work many years longer before he could consider retirement. In the end, they're betting that keeping him on for lower wages and a demotion will drive him to seek employment elsewhere or show his hand. Meanwhile, his days are numbered.

They have placed a discreet advertisement for a replacement."

"I see." She pondered this new information. "One thing is clear. Whoever is behind the ransacking would have the address book in their possession. Row me over to Grand Forks. We can have a look around while Ryan is romancing my cousin."

"You honestly think my childhood friend is behind this?" Jack fairly spluttered. "Why? What possible motive could he have?"

"To make the Sagamore look bad so he can have more business at Grand Forks Hotel and Cottages."

"Why would he want Mrs. VanDyne's address book?"

"You're the lawyer." She laughed. How could he not see what she saw? "Ryan wants her address book because she's one of the most influential members of high society in New York and Boston. She knows everyone. He could send post cards to those addresses and invite all the best sorts of people to his hotel. People with money to spend could turn Grand Forks into a success if he could find a way to leverage the finer points about the Steeles' hotel in a nicely done marketing campaign."

Jack's brows furrowed, and a scowl formed on his face.

She touched his arm and gentled her tone. "I hope I'm wrong, but would it hurt to have a look around his cottage, and if we find nothing, obtain the key to Mr.

Rhodes's room? We need to inspect both to find out which man is behind these things. If we find nothing, we'll know we are on the wrong trail. Then we must look harder for other culprits."

"But you are suggesting we spy without a warrant. In some courts of law, the evidence would be inadmissible," he retorted. "Furthermore, Ryan is my friend, and I am insulted you would think so ill of him. You've let your grandmother influence you."

Abby sighed. "I'm not suggesting we remove the evidence, but the police could be notified and obtain a warrant. I realize he's your friend, but don't you want to know the truth?"

"You have already convicted him. You can't know if your thoughts are true before he is proven guilty." Jack sounded indignant, and—she hated to say it—self-righteous.

Abby's chest heaved as she sat up straighter. "Don't twist your legal jargon around me, Jackson Gable. I may not be a lawyer, but I know the law well enough. All I'm suggesting is we have a look around. 'Tis merely a suggestion of how to discover the truth, and you know it." When he sulked, she grew impatient. "I'd like you to take me home."

Jack picked up the oars and steered the boat toward Green Island. Each time he brought the oars down into the lake, she could feel his anger. Some of his rowing even splashed her. Fine. If he wanted to remain blind, let him sulk and go on never knowing if his friend had caused the incidents. This didn't have to become one of her problems, anyhow. She had allowed herself to become too attached to Jack and his precious Sagamore.

When they reached the island, it didn't look as beautiful to Abby as when she'd first arrived. Jack tied the boat to the dock and climbed out while she hiked up her skirts and scrambled onto the dock without assistance. He turned to offer her a hand up, but surprise registered on his face when he realized she'd managed. Coming face-to-face, she navigated around him and proceeded toward the path leading up the island's hill. He followed closely behind with their untouched picnic basket.

A bellhop running downhill toward them stopped them in their tracks. Breathless, he explained, "Excuse me, Mr. Gable, but you have an urgent phone call at the main house from someone named Myra. The switchboard operator is holding the line for you because I saw you disembark when the call came in. Would you like to take it?"

Jack nodded, a brow rising. "Myra? Yes, I'll be right there."

"Ugh! Go talk to your Myra." More irritated than ever, Abby stomped her foot and whirled around. Myra? Who was Myra, anyway? Probably a girl in Philadelphia or someone he'd met at Harvard. How nice of him not to mention it until now.

Jack mumbled something in reply, but Abby didn't

hear it. She had quickened her pace to return to her villa. She didn't need him to accompany her to Grand Forks or anywhere. Seething, she arrived at the villa and paused at the front door to compose herself. She drew in a deep breath, swiped away the tears in her eyes, and tilted her chin. She would not cry over the end of a mere summer crush.

CHAPTER 17

The commandments, "You shall not commit adultery," "You shall not murder," "You shall not steal," "You shall not covet," and whatever other command there may be, are summed up in this one command: "Love your neighbor as yourself."

— ROMANS 13:9

*A*bby wasted no time on tears for Jack. Tears would come later when she laid her head on the pillow. For now, she needed to row across Lake George before Ryan returned to Grand Forks, perhaps in the same boat Jack had used to take her out on the lake.

If Ryan encountered her, she would need an excuse. Delivering an amorous message from her cousin should work. She wrote a love note to Ryan and signed it, *Eliza-*

beth. Dear Lord, forgive me. She tucked it inside the reticule matching her rose-pink dress and repinned the straw hat she'd worn for the outing with Jack. Such a shame to waste a lovely ensemble on someone who didn't appreciate her. No matter. She still needed to learn the truth for Elizabeth's sake.

It would cause alarm if she went out rowing by herself, so she settled on convincing Catherine to accompany her.

She went across the hall to plead with her sister who had been manicuring her nails. "Come with me on an excursion, Katie-bug. I need to investigate a matter, no questions asked. Can I trust you?"

"What are you up to, Abigail? You seldom get into any trouble. It must be serious." Her sister studied her. Then her face broke into a grin. "This sounds intriguing and exactly the distraction I need since Edwin must have afternoon tea with his family today. I'll get my hat."

They hurried to the boat and rowed across the George, walking until they reached Grand Forks. Hiding in the shrubbery, Abby and Catherine tried to guess which cottage belonged to Ryan. After peering in a number of wrong windows, they found his cottage by recognizing Ryan's old pair of riding boots drying out on the porch. Cute gingham valances hung in the windows, and window boxes filled with petunias adorned the home. It did not look like a villain's home.

Peering inside the front room, she saw a fireplace, a

small table with a red-and-white-checked tablecloth, a wooden hutch with some dishes, and two rocking chairs. A writing desk sat beneath one of the windows. A door led to a bedroom with a quilt spread on the bed. It looked remarkably tidy for a bachelor. A hotel cleaning lady must keep everything in order.

"What are we looking for?" Catherine whispered. "Does this have anything to do with Mrs. VanDyne's address book?"

"Yes, it does." Abby stepped away from the window and tried the door, hoping to find the dwelling empty of any persons. Unlocked, the knob turned, and the door opened. She crossed to the desk under the window and began pulling drawers out, rummaging through the contents.

"I'll peek in the hutch," Catherine offered.

"Sure." In the second drawer, she located what appeared to be an address book bound in brown leather. Far too manly for Mrs. VanDyne and certainly not the handwriting of a lady. She opened the third drawer and gasped.

Catherine whirled from the hutch. "What?"

"The coral shawl!" Beneath it lay a stack of letters tied with a ribbon and a gold book with an embossed design on a cream background and matching gold pen. Inside the cover, the words, *This book belongs to* were typeset above the signature line—which bore Mrs. Hazel VanDyne's signature. Her hands trembled and her heart sank. Why would Ryan hide his own family heirloom and claim it stolen? She could understand why he'd stolen the address book, but why his own great-grandmother's shawl?

Catherine, aghast, watched Abby return everything to the drawer the way she'd found the items. Closing the drawer, Abby sighed. "We can leave now. I found what we needed to know."

"But the shawl! And shouldn't we return the address book and letters to Mrs. VanDyne? Should we tell his parents what's happening?" Catherine posed good questions.

"If we return the address book and letters ourselves, we risk being accused of the crime. The same could be said for the shawl. We should inform the police so they can obtain a warrant or do whatever the state of New York requires."

"Right you are," Catherine agreed. "Sounds like something your beloved attorney would suggest. Say, why isn't Jack here helping you? I thought you said he likes mysteries."

"We're having a lover's spat."

The front door they'd purposely left ajar creaked the rest of the way open. "Who is having a lover's spat?" Ryan stepped inside his cottage.

"Oh, goodness, Ryan!" Abby breathed, her hand fluttering to her heart. Recovering quickly, she drew in a deep breath. "Hello, there. H-how nice to find you are home, after all. I was just telling Catherine how in love Elizabeth is with you, but Jack and I are quarreling."

"In love with me? Did she say that?" His suspicious gaze melted to curiosity.

"Well, yes, I almost forgot why we are here." A nervous little laugh escaped her. "Catherine and I wanted to see Grand Forks again. It's such a beautiful property. In any case, Elizabeth asked us to deliver one of those mushy love letters on her behalf. You know, the kind one wouldn't want our grandmother to find." She affected a sly wink.

"Sure." He nodded, though a question lingered in the word.

"Elizabeth is too shy to tell you in person. Seeing as you weren't home, we thought we'd leave it for you on your desk. Being a writer, I had to stand here a moment and admire what a lovely view you have from this window. And Catherine was just commenting on how terribly neat your cottage is." She pulled the letter out of her reticule as she spoke, handing it to him. "Since you are here now, we can give it to you personally."

Ryan eyed them both and then accepted the page. He unfolded the note, glancing at it. He cleared his throat. "I'll read this later. Have you been here long?" He refolded the note and stuffed it into his shirt pocket.

"No, in fact, not long enough to even remove our hats. We thought about sitting down at the table to wait for you," Catherine added. Too chatty. "It's such a charming cottage. Is it a one-bedroom or do you have two bedrooms?"

"This is a one-bedroom, but I plan to build on

someday, maybe." He removed his hat and holding the brim, turned it around and around in his hands. "Some of the others are two-bedroom cottages."

"I see. Well, it's a lovely property. We should be getting back, or Gran will scold us." Abby stepped toward the door. "Will we see you this evening? I think Grandmother said we're going to the steak restaurant. Everyone raves about the skillet-fried steak and mushrooms."

Ryan stepped aside as they progressed onto the porch. "Yes, I came home to change out of these clothes. Elizabeth and I were out riding horses and picnicking with the earl and Tybalt. Augusta joined us and Miss Caroline Bernard, the companion for Mrs. Lloyd's daughters. Some of them plan to meet us at the steak place."

"Ah. Well, I'm sure you want time to dress. We'll see you this evening." Abby smiled. "Remember, please don't mention our visit tonight. We wouldn't want Grandmother to find out about that mushy letter."

"Mum is the word." Ryan made a pinching motion over his lips.

They hurried away, Abby's heart pumping from the unexpected encounter. She could feel Ryan staring after them as they re-traced their footsteps to the main road leading to the dock.

When they reached the shore, Catherine paused to catch her breath while Abby untied the rowboat from the dock. "It's a good thing you brought that letter, but as soon as Elizabeth tells him she didn't send it, he's going to do something rash. He'll know we're on to him."

"I know. I should have waited for Jack," Abby confessed as they stepped into the boat, careful not to tip or drag their skirts in the lake. "I'll think of something."

"*I* think we need to go to the police with what we know."

Abby hesitated before pushing the boat away from the dock. "Just help me row and I'll think about it. Maybe after dinner I'll know what to do."

CHAPTER 18

It was rapture enough just to sit there beside him in silence, alone in the summer night in the white splendor of moonshine, with the wind blowing down on them out of the pine woods.

— L.M. MONTGOMERY, *THE BLUE CASTLE*

*A*bby dressed in a gray-and-black satin evening gown, donning her pearl necklace. The bolo jacket boasted puffed sleeves with ruffles along the neckline and a black silk band cinched the waist of the dress. She wanted to look her best for Jack to remind him what he would miss if he returned to this Myra. Slipping into her cream shoes, she headed downstairs.

Grandmother had arranged for a carriage to drive

them to the restaurant. They climbed inside, but Abby could barely enjoy the ride—or the meal that followed.

She had made a mess of things with Jack. He sat at the large, round table with them, but they barely acknowledged each other. Probably dwelling on thoughts of Myra, for one thing.

Making matters worse, when Ryan arrived and took a seat beside Elizabeth, he gave Abby and Catherine odd glances throughout the meal. While every bite of the steak tasted delicious, and Grandmother kept the conversation flowing, Abby could hardly wait to return to the villa. What should she do? She wanted to tell Jack about her discovery, but how could she when he refused to speak to her?

Decidedly ill about the whole matter, Abby endured a ride to the main house, where the men frequently gathered after meals to read newspapers in the drawing room and the ladies retreated to the round turret parlor for discussion, reading, or embroidery. After ten minutes, she'd demonstrated enough restraint and social etiquette for the evening. She needed fresh air and a walk to the villa to clear her mind.

"I'll walk home, Gran. I need the exercise," Abby whispered.

Gran looked up from her conversation with Ava. "Certainly. We'll be along shortly. We're talking about next summer."

Ava smiled and reached out to pat Abby on the hand. "I noticed you and Jack are having trouble in paradise. It will work out. I used to have spats with my husband before he passed, God rest his soul."

The gesture only provided the reverse effect. If Ava had noticed she and Jack had issues, then everyone else had too. She bit her tongue and offered a polite, "Thank you, Mrs. Lewis." Nodding toward Blanche, Abby slipped out of the parlor. "Good night, ladies."

A glance into the long drawing room off the foyer told her Ryan, Jack, the earl, Tybalt, and several other gentlemen appeared engaged in conversation, many others engrossed in reading the newspapers delivered by steamship. She could make her escape in peace, despite the darkness that had descended upon Green Island.

Once outside, she could breathe again. Maybe she could find a quiet place in the woods to sit and pray. She needed the Lord's wisdom, time to think things through, and a place to have a good cry. Abby cut a path through the woods on her right. How had she missed the fact Jack had a girlfriend until now?

Tears began to pool in her eyes, but she kept walking, the weight of the world on her heart. A while later, a twig snapped somewhere behind her. No doubt just a squirrel scurrying away. She kept going, quickening her pace.

If Ryan planned to do nothing more than borrow Mrs. VanDyne's address book, would it seem silly to go to the police if he had nothing to do with the other things occurring at Sagamore? What if Jack dragged his feet because he would never want the board of investors and the owner of the resort to prosecute his friend? On the other hand, what if Ryan took even more drastic actions against the Sagamore in the future?

Another twig snapped. It seemed so close, Abby hiked up her satin skirts and began to run, careful of her steps to avoid falling or twisting her ankle. Easier said than done in the dark with only the moonlight. Best to slip behind a large oak tree and hide.

Footsteps crunched on leaves and more twigs. Heavy footsteps, as if they belonged to a man. Another set of footsteps came from a different direction. A branch snapped in the same area, but the first steps she'd heard now seemed to run away.

Then a voice called out from the area where she'd heard the second set of footsteps. "Abby? Are you out here, Abby?"

She breathed a sigh of relief. "Jack? I'm over here." She stepped out from behind the tree, looking for him, shaking, tears in her eyes.

Jack emerged from the thick trees to her left, and she collapsed in his arms, the tears streaming down her face. "Someone was following me."

He pulled her close, wiping her tears away. "Don't cry. I know. I saw Ryan say goodnight to Elizabeth and follow you outside. When I asked Elizabeth if she knew where you'd gone, she said she assumed you were walking to the villa. She said Ryan had to check on his mother, who needs an expensive operation. That's when I knew I'd been a fool and should have listened to you. I decided to follow Ryan. I think I made enough noise to scare him away."

She nodded. "Jack, I don't know what to do. Catherine and I went to Grand Forks this afternoon after you brought me back to Green Island. I know you didn't want me to go, and now I wish I would have listened. I think he knows we're onto him. We found Mrs. VanDyne's address book, her letters, and the shawl in the desk at his cottage, and then he walked in on us. I don't know about the commotion going on with the guests today, or who cut the saddle, but I do know Ryan is involved with the ransacking and has stolen his own family heirloom. At the very least, someone has framed him and placed the items in his desk."

Jack pressed a finger to her lips. "I know. My friend Myra told me some things."

"Myra? Jack, who is Myra?" Abby blinked in the dark, but not for long. Something caught her eye and Jack's attention, lighting up the main house of the Sagamore in the distance through the trees.

"Fire! The Sagamore is on fire!" Jack's mouth dropped open as the flames shot up around the main entrance of the resort.

"Oh, Jack. My family! They could still be inside!" Abby hiked up her skirts, and Jack grabbed her other hand. They ran as fast as she could in a satin evening gown with heels.

When they arrived on the edge of the lawn, the

flames had begun to encroach on the third floor. They watched in horror as the front porch made cracking noises and part of the porch roof fell, bringing a gust of flames with it. After spilling out from the French doors along the portico, guests huddled in groups all over the lawn. Others came from the rear of the building. Still others must've escaped through the kitchen door or their private terraces.

Someone reached the chapel and began ringing the church bell while men formed a line to pass water using buckets, pots, pans, and dishpans staff brought from the kitchen. The line stretched out from a red hand pump near the end of the portico to the main entrance where the fire raged. It appeared as if they contained the fire to the area between the breakfast room and the drawing room on either side of the foyer, but flames quickly consumed the porch. The wicked orange tongues clung to the building walls, trying to climb, scorching everything in their wake. All of this in mere minutes.

"Abby!" Catherine's voice called out, but Abby couldn't find her family in the chaos. The blinding light of the growing fire caused her to blink at the darkness hovering over the front lawn and the frightened faces of guests.

Jack pointed to Grandmother, Elizabeth, Catherine, Ava, and Blanche huddled near a flowerbed in the middle of the lawn. Abby sighed with relief. Augusta and her family gazed at the fire from nearby, faces slack with horror.

Jack pulled Abby along to unite her with her family. "I'll return when we have the fire out."

Abby nodded as he took off to join the earl, Tybalt, Beau Destin, Mr. Rhodes, and many other men helping to contain and extinguish the fire. She hadn't even had a chance to say goodbye to him. Would he be safe?

A while later, firefighters and police officers swarmed the Sagamore in horse-drawn wagons, ringing their bells. Abby prayed, squeezing her sister's hand as they watched the firemen join the fight to defeat the blaze. Catherine caught her up to speed, explaining how Tybalt had seen the flames first, alerted everyone, and together with the manager and staff, began emptying the main house of its guests. Thankfully, most of the resort's patrons had gathered on the first floor, but scouring every room and suite for guests took time.

Finally, the men managed to extinguish the flames. Mr. Rhodes began helping Beau account for each guest while the firemen attempted to assess structural damage. Not far from the front entrance, Jack and some guests Abby knew to be a honeymooning couple spoke with the police. About five minutes more passed before he returned, pulling her aside.

What Jack had been about to tell her about Myra lingered in the back of her mind, but the most pressing question demanded to be voiced first. "Were you talking with the police about Ryan?"

He nodded, accepting a cup of coffee from one of the kitchen staff. Turning to her, he asked, "Would you like a cup of coffee?"

"Coffee? Yes, please!" Abby accepted the cup Jack handed her before the waiter moved on. The delicious smell coming from their paper cups revived her and Jack.

Jack continued in a low voice. "I need to lead the police to the evidence. I promised I would help in any way I could. We'll be leaving shortly to cross the George and bring Ryan in. I've told them all we know, and that couple spotted him setting fire to the Sagamore. He must have done it after I scared him out of the woods. They have probable cause now and won't need a warrant."

She almost choked on her sip of coffee. "Wait, did you say someone saw Ryan do this?"

"Yes, the honeymooning couple saw him from their balcony. Want to stroll down closer to the lake for a few minutes?"

"Sure." The news he gave her made her sad for Jack, not to mention Elizabeth.

Abby followed Jack down the hill of the front lawn to the banks of Lake George. They sat on the edge of the dock, dangling their feet above the water.

She studied his tightly set profile in the moonlight, hesitant to probe into his emotions about Ryan too soon. Best to take things slow. They were both still shaken. "Did you learn how badly the hotel is damaged?"

"The main house appears safe so far, but the front porch will need replaced, and the scorched stucco walls refaced." Jack also informed her the firemen continued to check for structural safety to determine if guests could return to their lodgings. He added, "Some guests may be angry enough to leave tomorrow."

Abby grimaced. "I suppose it's possible. At least the fire didn't reach any of their rooms."

Jack sipped some coffee and then continued. "I am terribly sorry, Abby. I owe you a huge apology. I hope you can forgive me. I was blinded by my friendship with Ryan. Myra is a fellow journalist. She writes a social column. Someone contacted her by telephone and offered an anonymous scoop about the Sagamore to destroy our reputation, just as you suspected. The man mentioned robberies, poor service, disgruntled patrons, and faulty tack. Myra isn't going to run the story as a favor to me, and she is not and has never been a romantic interest. She's fifteen years my senior."

"That's a relief on both counts, but especially the part about not running the story," Abby said, but inside, she wanted to jump for joy to discover Jack didn't have a sweetheart named Myra. How silly of her to think such a thought in the first place. "Of course, I forgive you."

"The problem is, we don't know how many other newspaper reporters Ryan may have contacted. But we believe Sagamore's reputation is solid enough to with-stand the hiccup."

"It's all starting to make sense." Abby sighed.

"Between the evidence you saw and the witnesses to him setting the fire, and motive enough, maybe even a confession..." Jack choked up on those words.

"Why do you suppose he took the shawl and claimed it stolen?"

"To throw us off his trail."

She touched his hand. "I'm so sorry, Jack. I'm also concerned for his mother. I'm sure there are ways we could help her. I wish he'd have come to us for help. We could have hosted a fundraiser with our connections. Secondly, I should have waited for you before conducting my own search. I guess the Lord is showing my stubborn, independent heart that two are better than one." Abby sipped more of her coffee. "Maybe he wouldn't have resorted to starting the fire if I'd left things alone."

"I think he's desperate enough to do just about anything, no matter who it hurts." Jack drank the rest of the contents of his cup and set it aside, rising, then helping her up as well. "When tonight is over, and the police have Ryan in their custody, I'd like to ask if you'd allow me to escort you to the Grand Summer Farewell Ball, where I plan to make it one of the best nights of your life—I mean, of our lives, I hope."

Had he implied a forthcoming marriage proposal? The approaching police officers signaled their readiness to pursue the suspect. Her heart thumping, she hurried to respond. "Of course, you may escort me to the ball, so come back to me safe."

"I will. I promise. Pray for us. We need it." Jack pulled her into his arms while the police began boarding a yacht.

Abby held onto his shirt collar with both hands, returning a passionate kiss. She didn't care who saw them, not even if the police rolled their eyes. In that moment, she knew she loved this man and couldn't live without him. Before releasing him, she added, "I don't know if I can wait for the Grand Summer Farewell Ball."

He smiled, squeezing her hand gently, his blue eyes sparkling before he hurried away. By morning, she hoped all would be right again in their world.

CHAPTER 19

For where envying and strife is, there is confusion
and every evil work.

— JAMES 3:16

*A*bby would have hardly slept except fatigue
had taken its toll. She whispered a prayer for
Jack's safety, thanking God no lives had been lost due to
the fire. Closing her eyes, she fell into a deep sleep,
waking at nearly eleven o'clock the next morning. The
world felt different. Her heart soared with hope that
somehow overnight, all the world had been put to right
again.

She couldn't remember when she'd slept so late.
Dressing in a pale yellow frock, she hurried downstairs
to find her family eating brunch on the terrace with
Jack, the earl, and Tybalt. Lord Monroe and Tybalt sat

in chairs holding cups of tea in saucers, apart from the table but drawn up close to her sister, Elizabeth, Gran, and Jack as they finished eating. An empty seat and table setting beside Jack appeared to be reserved for her.

"Jack, you're safe!" she breathed as he patted the seat.

He returned her smile, looking just as happy to see her. "Good morning, sunshine. Your grandmother ordered breakfast for us."

Gran leaned toward her. "There are scrambled eggs, bacon, fresh fruit, and a few more waffles on the cart."

"I'll fix you a plate," Catherine offered, setting about the task.

"Thank you." Abby blinked in the warm sunshine as she focused on Jack. "How did things go last night?" She shot a glance at Elizabeth, who was quietly sipping her juice. Poor thing. She'd surely heard the news by now.

"As well as could be expected." Jack answered in a low voice. "Ryan didn't try to hide at all. It was the oddest thing. We found him at his cottage. He acted as if he didn't know what they were talking about when the police questioned him at first, but when I found the address book, the letters, and the shawl in his desk and handed them to one of the officers, his confession tumbled out. The fire, the ransacking, cutting the saddle, confusing our employees by disrupting their work and delivering false messages...he confessed he'd done all of those things to make the Sagamore look bad. Along with it, a stream of sickeningly jealous, bitter talk when he looked at me. He went on and on about how I'd had it too easy, and he'd had it too hard."

"He'd hate someone like me," the earl remarked. "But people don't realize everyone has problems, even those born into privilege."

Tybalt nodded. "With privilege comes greater responsibility."

Jack continued. "Ryan will likely go to prison for a very long time. Too many people could have died in the fire, and the saddle incident could have killed someone as well. I feel as though I failed to help my friend before he fell into these thought patterns, but with the demands of law school, how could I have known?"

Murmurs of agreement and sympathy answered his query.

Grandmother added, "You mustn't blame yourself, Jack. I'm sure God has a plan to reform Ryan. He needs this time to reconsider his ways."

"Thank you, Mrs. Wiltshire." Jack offered her a faint smile. "I still like Abby's idea about hosting a fundraiser for Ryan's mother so she can have the operation she needs."

"My granddaughter has a heart of gold." Gran poured some creamer into her coffee and stirred, smiling at Abby. "All three of them do."

"I'll speak to my father to see if we can make it

happen. Maybe at the Grand Summer Farewell Ball." Jack reached for more bacon.

"I shall be among the first to contribute." The earl sat up straighter and adjusted his tie.

"I'm sure my family will as well," Tybalt's brows furrowed as he rubbed his chin, contemplating the matter. "In addition to some funds for her operation, we'll send some tender beef roasts and steak to their hotel. Texans like to be generous."

"Maybe things will calm down around here now," Catherine tucked a stray brunette curl into her grown-up Gibson Girl hairstyle. "I just want to enjoy that fancy pool and wear my new swimming attire. No one else has anything like Sagamore's bathing pool except some place in Philadelphia I read about in a newspaper."

Jack grinned. "Now you know where my father and the board got their idea. We are based out of Philadelphia. Mark my words, Father will have a construction company out here before the week is out. They'll have the repairs from the fire done in a matter of a few weeks."

Gran looked at Catherine. "You just need to remember to stay on the girls' side of the pool, young lady."

"Yes, ma'am," Catherine replied as they laughed.

Jack turned to Abby. "We came along about an hour ago to tell you all the news and ask if you wanted to go to the yacht party to view the regatta shipside this evening. That's when I discovered my sleeping beauty had yet to rise and your grandmother invited us to stay for brunch."

Abby blushed. "I am usually an early riser, but if it means breakfast on the terrace in the company of these handsome heroes, I don't mind sleeping in more often. I shall be delighted to accompany you to the yacht party this evening, Jackson. I'm sure it will cheer us up."

"Yes, you all put the fire out so quickly. The Sagamore is blessed to have the three of you," Elizabeth commented as tears brimmed in her eyes. "I am shocked and horrified to learn of Ryan's behavior. It's going to take my heart a long time to recover. I shall never believe myself a capable judge of one's character ever again. I should have listened to you, Gran."

"I shall not argue with this newfound wisdom." Gran patted Elizabeth's hand. "It has come at a high price, but your heart will recover in time. This, too, shall pass."

Elizabeth sniffled and dabbed at the corners of her eyes with her handkerchief. "At least the Lord gave me a mountain moment as a model."

"Perhaps a little attention from a gentleman across the pond is what this dear girl needs." Lord Monroe shifted in his seat. "Miss Parker, if you would consider it, I shall be happy to escort you to the yacht party. Tybalt has obtained permission to court Miss Augusta, so I fear I am without a companion unless you will have me."

Elizabeth looked up, her lips parting. She quickly

recovered, sitting up straighter. "How kind of you, Lord Monroe. Yes, I would be delighted. I may not be a very talkative companion, however. I still bear this weight in my heart, and although I know I shall live, it may take me a little while before I am my usual chipper self."

"Of course. If you were too chatty after such a tragic circumstance, I would think you a heartless damsel," Lord Monroe confessed, making everyone laugh. Studying Elizabeth, he grinned when she smiled at his joke.

CHAPTER 20

Love recognizes no barriers. It jumps hurdles, leaps
fences, penetrates walls to arrive at its destination
full of hope.

— MAYA ANGELOU

The rest of the summer progressed like a
warm, caressing breeze. An enormous
construction team repaired the damages to the resort in
an astonishing fourteen days. Guests of the Sagamore
enjoyed picnics, swimming, tennis, badminton, and
croquet. August brought Friday evening dances, nature
hikes on the mainland, crochet club, church services,
painting on the lawn from easels, and even an outdoor
banquet complete with lanterns and greenery on linen-
covered tables. They went on more horseback rides,

read books on the new front porch, and glided across Lake George in yachts and rowboats. Romances blossomed, friends exchanged addresses before going home.

Jack and Abby enjoyed August immensely despite the intensity of the heat and muggy weather. She finished her memoir, *Azusa*. He finished *Trindle Castle: A Scottish Mystery*. They exchanged manuscripts and proofread each other's work.

"I was hoping I could find all sorts of things to correct for you, but it's done so well—in fact, brilliantly done, my darling." Jack's blue eyes shone in the afternoon sunshine as they sat on the porch of his villa on the last Monday of August. "My hopes of critiquing your work with my own experience and telling you all the scenes you need to rewrite are dashed."

"Well, your mystery had me hooked, pulling me in from beginning to end. I turned the pages as fast as I could." Abby handed him his manuscript. "I found only one miniscule plot hole, and I loved your characters. They reminded me of us. Suggested edits are in pencil."

"Thank you. Your grammar is better than mine," he admitted. "I put my few suggestions in pencil for you too."

"That's quite a compliment coming from a Harvard grad." Abby grinned beneath her wide-brimmed straw hat and the scarf holding it to her head, basking in his praise.

"I'm going to do a newspaper article plugging your book as soon as you find a publisher."

"But Jack—"

He held up a hand. "Nothing you can say will stop me."

She smiled. "You'll let me read it first?"

"Oh, now you don't trust me?" he teased.

She elbowed him, and after a great deal of tickling and chasing her into his villa's sitting room where Elizabeth, Lord Monroe, Tybalt, and Augusta danced to records from Augusta's personal collection playing on a phonograph they'd borrowed from the Sagamore, they fell into a dance to "In the Shade of the Old Apple Tree." Then Elizabeth played "By the Light of the Silvery Moon," and they swayed with Abby's cheek resting against Jack's strong shoulder.

She could hardly wait until the night of the Grand Summer Farewell Ball. Would he remain true to his promise to provide the happiest night of her life? The wait kept her in agony. She dared not voice her thoughts since she'd never allowed herself to hope for anyone to ask for her hand in marriage, and she didn't want to do anything to ruin her destiny. Then she would chide herself, for who could close doors God Himself chose to open for His beloved children?

*O*n the late afternoon before the Grand Summer Farewell Ball, Abby stood before the oval full-length mirror in the villa. Her peach ballgown had short, puffed sleeves, a square neckline, a natural waist embellished with a slim peach velvet ribbon, and a demi train. It looked lovely with the long white evening gloves and white ankle boots with low heels. Her hair swept into a fashionable style resembling the Gibson Girls, and elegant pearl combs in her hair complemented her pearl necklace and gold earbobs.

Abby's family would join them at the ball following a grand couples' promenade on the portico. Jack would fetch her early since he said he had a surprise planned. As she gazed at her completed look one last time, she let out a sigh of contentment. How everyone had changed and grown that summer at Sagamore.

Elizabeth had learned her lesson about placing her affection on a gentleman based on her expectations of his wealth and status, and now she had a blossoming romance with Lord Monroe. Ryan had broken her heart, but the earl would escort her to the ball, making her the envy of all the other marriageable ladies on the island. Ryan faced a long prison sentence because of his jealousy, but Jack had followed through on his promise to help the family, making arrangements for patrons to donate at the ball for Mrs. Steele's operation. Everyone prayed Ryan would seek repentance and forgiveness for his actions and mend his ways in the years ahead.

Catherine's effort to be patient had borne fruit. Tonight, Edwin would escort her to the ball, and tomorrow, his family would leave on the steamship, but they had already exchanged addresses.

Tybalt Monroe had become engaged to Augusta a week ago, and her growing friendship with Abby had begun to transform her into a kinder, gentler version of herself. She had begun reading God's Word on a regular basis and frequently spoke to Abby about it.

Most of all, Abby herself had come a long way—from pursuing her own desire to remain independent to embracing God's will for her to marry Jack. Should he propose tonight and she pledge to become his wife as she hoped, she could rest assured that he would never clip her wings.

Jack had learned things too. Some people did not stay the same, for one thing. You had to keep an open line of communication with those you cared about, to make certain they were truly okay. He'd also told Abby how much her faith in the Lord inspired and deepened his.

Mr. Rhodes had redeemed himself in some ways by helping put the fire out at Sagamore, but he'd announced his retirement. Probably for the best.

Then the knock on the door came, and Catherine announced Jack's arrival. "He's waiting for you downstairs, Abby. He brought a dozen peach roses to match your evening gown, and a buggy is outside."

"Thank you, Katie-bug." Abby descended the staircase while Jack drank in her appearance with an approving eye as he held the bouquet of roses. When she reached his side, he slipped his arm around her waist. "You look stunning, Abby." He handed her the roses, and she smiled, breathing in the fragrant blooms.

"You don't look so bad yourself." She admired his smart black tailcoat and white vest as they held hands and walked outside to the buggy. He lifted her into the seat and then climbed into the driver's seat beside her.

"Where are we going?" she asked as he picked up the reins. "I'm dying of curiosity."

"It's a mystery." But he handed her an envelope.

"Haven't we solved our share of those?" She raised a brow as she inspected the envelope. It smelled of his musky cologne, making her dizzy as she inhaled the fragrance mingling with that of her roses.

"Tonight, you'll have a few clues to each destination. Open the first and tell me where we're going."

She smiled, opening the envelope and drawing out the note. She unfolded and read it, a smirk dancing about her lips. "*Clue number one: Our first kiss happened here.*" She turned to look at him. "That's easy. I'd never forget the place. We're going to the spot where you found me reading in the meadow up on the crest overlooking the stables."

"Very good." He snapped the reins, and in short order, they arrived at the location. He drew the team to a stop, came around to her side, and helped her down. "Do you see the next clue?"

She studied the area. "I see a ribbon with another envelope dangling from the tree over there." Without waiting for direction, she hurried to it, snatched the envelope, and unfolded the note inside. She glanced at Jack. He observed her enthusiasm with the same debonair smile he'd worn the first time she saw him standing on the front porch of the Sagamore. She lowered her gaze to read the note. "It says, *Please say you'll marry me. I love you with all of my heart.*" Her voice wobbled, but she drew a breath to continue. "*It may be a little crazy, two writers living in wedded bliss together, but I will do my best to make you happy for the rest of our lives. P.S. If your answer is yes, the next clue is in front of you.*"

She looked up to find him kneeling before her on bended knee, holding another envelope. Joy overflowed into laughter. "Yes, Jack. I'll marry you. At least we know what we're getting into. Writers are difficult, indeed."

He chuckled as she withdrew the envelope in his hand. She read the note out loud. "*Turn around to find the next clue.*" Abby glanced at him and then over her shoulder. She didn't see anything at first, but then she took a few steps, moving some full branches to see a line of rose petals strewn on the ground. Jack followed as the petals led her to a clearing with a linen-covered round table for two. Nearing the table, she let out a soft gasp. Three smaller bowls of more peach roses surrounded a flickering lantern. A wheeled cart beside the table held a number of covered plates, and a covered plate sat on one side of the table. He'd done all this for her?

"Jack, this is so romantic," she said on an exhaled breath.

"I think you'll find the next clue under the lid of the plate over your dish."

She lifted and set aside the lid, and a beautiful diamond ring glittered at her from an open velvet box. "Oh!" she squealed, her hands flying to her mouth. "It's lovely!"

"Try it on."

She removed her gloves, plucked the ring from the box, and slid the diamond ring on her finger. Then they stood there for a moment and admired how it sparkled in the sunshine. "It's beautiful. Thank you, Jack. I will cherish it forever as a symbol of our love."

He smiled, drawing her into his arms. "Now it's time to sit together and eat our first meal as betrothed, and you can tell me your dreams for our wedding. I shall tell you about asking your grandmother's permission for your hand, and then telephoning your father. Then we will go to the promenade in style in the carriage and dance the night away."

She giggled, covering her mouth with her hands, trying to imagine this. "You telephoned my father?"

He nodded. "I did. Well, your grandmother placed the call and handed me the telephone. He said the wedding can be this November. He was very clear it should be at the church you've attended all of your life in Cincinnati. He'll be happy to walk you down the aisle, give you away, and then perform the ceremony, since he is the pastor, after all."

"Did you break the news gently to your parents about our being Presbyterian, Sherlock?" She tilted her chin up with a teasing smirk.

"All in good time, my dear." He winked. "I sent them a telegram that I'm proposing tonight to a preacher's daughter on Sagamore, and they're looking forward to meeting you before November, Miss Watson."

"I guess everyone is on board for a November wedding. Grandmother will say it's barely enough time to have my dress made."

"That's precisely what she said when she heard your father said November." He chuckled, and she broke into a fit of giggles, nodding.

Gathering her composure, she sighed, breathing in the bliss and joy of what seemed like the Kingdom of God come down to earth. Certainly, it had, but after tonight, she might have to pinch herself and stare at her wedding ring for a few days while they journeyed to Cincinnati. Yes, a November wedding couldn't happen soon enough. They'd telephone each other every single day until then. Parting from him for even a few weeks seemed troubling, but soon they would be together forever.

"Jack, you really are a dream come true. If we can dance away the rest of our lives together, I am the happiest girl in all the world."

"And I am the happiest man in all the world with you in my arms."

Abby smiled as he drew her closer for another sweet kiss. "What a summer at Sagamore this has been."

"What a summer at Sagamore, indeed!"

The End

Did you enjoy this book? We hope so!
**Would you take a quick minute to leave a review
where you purchased the book?**
It doesn't have to be long. Just a sentence or two telling
what you liked about the story!

Receive a FREE ebook and get updates when new Wild
Heart books release: https://wildheartbooks.org/
newsletter

Don't miss the next book in Romance at the Gilded Age
Resorts Series!

A Season at the Grand
By Sherri Wilson Johnson

POINT CLEAR, ALABAMA
1905

Amelia Harris stepped off the *Baldwin* with one
gloved hand in the porter's hand and the other grip-
ping the handle of her camera case. She could not
afford for either of them to land in Mobile Bay. If she
lost her camera, then her summer in Point Clear
would end before it began, also terminating her

career with *The Photographic Times*. They had sent her here to capture nature photographs as well as images of the elite guests enjoying their seaside holiday, and she couldn't allow any mishaps to derail her assignment.

Besides, the summer here enjoying the same luxuries of the wealthy meant a reprieve from the matchmaking of Aunt Polly and Aunt Patsy. Why did they insist her marriageable years had an expiration date and that her occupation as a photographer would damage not only her reputation but her future, as well? Why did they think a woman only twenty-five years old couldn't still find a husband?

"Miss?" The porter's voice snapped her out of her rumination.

With a quick nod and a prayer her embarrassment hadn't touched her cheeks more than the June heat already had, she smiled, then released his hand. "Thank you, sir."

"My pleasure. Enjoy your stay at the Grand Hotel. Your belongings will arrive in your room shortly."

Amelia smoothed her left hand across her stomach and breathed a sigh. As though that would calm the butterflies which flooded inside her. What did she have to be anxious about? While this might be her first assignment this far from home and without a chaperone or colleague, she carried herself well among the elite and had nothing to fear. Besides, she was here to photograph, not to make friends. Her presence as a commissioned photographer required no further burden of proof.

With *The Photographic Times* expecting a minimum of two thousand nature images for their penny post-cards, socializing sat at the bottom of her priority stack. Best she decide right now to pack her jitters away in her trunk along with her swimwear and leave them there all summer.

Pressing her shoulders against the coastal humidity, she took a step down the boardwalk toward her awaiting adventure.

"Jimmy, come back here. No running on the board-walk, young man," a woman's stern voice called from behind Amelia.

Before she could peek over her shoulder for a hint at the commotion, a boy—Jimmy, most likely—broke through the cluster of guests and slammed into her, ripping her case from her hand.

"Oh no!" She fell to her knees on the weathered boardwalk and grasped the case seconds before it spun its way into the glistening bay. With her hat now dangling by its string across her back and her body splayed out on top of the leather case like a dead fish, she must already be the subject of the onlookers' gossip. Surely, it would be better if she reboarded the bay boat and returned to Philadelphia this instant.

"Miss, are you all right?" As a deep voice floated over her, heavy with obvious concern, she pushed off the case and attempted to stand.

But her shoe had entangled itself in the hem of her skirt, and she wasn't going anywhere without this gentleman's assistance.

"Here, allow me." He extended his hand to her.

With no choice, she placed her hand in his while raising her chin as she sucked in her embarrassment.

He helped her to her feet, her grasp on the case handle tighter than before.

When her gaze met his, she gulped.

Titus Overton? The general manager of the resort and one of the most eligible bachelors of the South held her hand. Of course, she would sprawl out in front of someone of his status.

He pointed his glassy stare at her, then smiled without showing his teeth, which would have been a difficult task with such a thick mustache resting on his upper lip. The portraits she'd seen of him in the society section of the newspaper hadn't revealed the blueness of his eyes, how even the waters of the Gulf of Mexico were no match for them. Nor had those images hinted at the sandiness of his hair. Indeed, it was as if he were made from the very nature that surrounded him.

Her belly did another flutter, which raced upward and took her heart prisoner.

No, no, no, you are here to work. Nothing else.

"Miss..."

She cleared her throat. "Yes, Miss Harris, Amelia Harris. I'm here with *The Photographic Times* by way of Philadelphia."

He nodded and released her hand. "Of course, well, if you are satisfactory now, stable on your feet, I'll let you proceed to the registration desk."

"Yes, yes, of course. I—well—there was a boy who pushed past me and ripped my camera case from my hand. I assure you, I am not a clumsy woman by nature."

"Under the circumstances, especially after being aboard a vessel for so long, I'd say you handled yourself quite gracefully. A lesser woman would have gone over the edge." He smiled again, little crinkles surrounding the outer corners of his eyes. "Titus Overton, general manager. Pleased to make your acquaintance. I'm certain we will see each other again. Do not hesitate to ask me if you need assistance with anything regarding your photography."

With cheeks ablaze and threatening to set her entire being afire, she gave another nod, then returned her hat to her head. Putting one foot in front of the other and steering clear of the edge, she marched away from what counted as her most humiliating experience to date.

Lord, please don't let this be an indication of how this summer will go. I need this assignment and the time away from home.

Miss Amelia Harris. From Philadelphia.

Titus watched her walk away, hands inside his suitcoat pockets, the warmth of her gloved hand still tingling on his.

Was it the heat that sucked every bit of moisture from his mouth and throat, or was it the flaxen-haired woman with the appropriate amount of pink gracing her cheeks? With eyes like sapphires in the most perfect almond shape, she could rule the entire world. If he guessed right about her, she had no clue about the lasting impression a first interaction with her made.

Titus swallowed—or at least tried to—as the traveling photographer disappeared into the main building. Would her accommodations be suitable enough for such a fine and lovely woman? For if she requested something different, something with a view of the bay, he'd make it happen. As manager of the resort, he could do that.

As the last of his forty new guests exited the boardwalk and followed the crushed-shell path to the hotel, Titus pivoted toward the bay and released his breath. The pelican on the post at the end had the right idea.

Freedom.

Landing wherever the wind took him.

Nothing tethering him to anything or anyone except his need for food.

Removing his hat, he retrieved his kerchief from his pocket, then wiped the sweat from his brow and the back of his neck. The summer's heat was only beginning. The start of the almost-endless noise from guests who would come and go throughout the season meant little peace for Titus. Little privacy. Scarce thinking time. No time for planning his future far away from the resort.

One day, he'd shed the obligations that came with managing the Grand Hotel, obligations Uncle Sidney had placed on him when Cousin Norman drowned at sea. Uncle Sidney's position on the board of directors and his greed assured his wishes came true. This time, at Titus's expense. Uncle Sidney had been so good to him during his formative years, but after losing Norman, he'd placed all the expectations he'd had of his son on Titus's shoulders. One day wouldn't be here soon enough.

After returning his hat to his head, he shoved his hands into his suitcoat pockets again with a sigh. If Titus didn't mind himself, this summer might also mean the end of his carefree days as an unattached man, if previous summers were any indication of the matchmaking that transpired when wealthy women took their holidays.

He'd vowed after losing Evelyn he'd never let his heart betray him again, never let his gaze admire a woman for more than a few moments. Just enough to give his heart that little lift of glee it needed every so often. That tingle that reminded him of love's purpose.

But then it had to stop there.

The *Baldwin* sputtered away from the boardwalk, and the last of his staff wheeled carts of trunks and luggage toward the hotel, leaving him alone with the pelican and his thoughts. Alone, that was, until the warm gulf breeze whipped across him, sending the pelican into the air and making Titus wish he could fly away with him.

His migratory bird research and his efforts to protect them, watching the males and females find their mates, build their nests, then start their families—was all he needed. Not the noise humans brought with them, not the heartbreak that accompanied entanglements.

Straightening his shoulders, he nodded to no one but himself and strengthened his resolve. His mission involved getting through this summer while searching for a replacement, then moving on to the work he really wanted to do—preserving nature and doing something that mattered. Unencumbered by a mate of his own. Free and limitless like the gulls and the pelicans.

No Miss Amelia Harris from Philadelphia would hinder his objectives. No, sir, she would not.

Amelia didn't mind that her room didn't face the bay, nor did she mind the simplicity of its furnishings. She'd spend most of her time outdoors photographing, anyway. As long as the bed brought support and comfort at the end of each day and didn't squeak or creak too much, she couldn't ask for more. Facing east, it would provide her with the rising sun each morning streaming through the window, which was all she needed for her prayer and Scripture time.

She might even take advantage of the seats beneath the moss-draped oaks twenty feet outside her door for her time with the Lord. She had much to thank Him for. First, over all, her safe travels and the unscathed equipment. Given the multiple trains she'd boarded plus the steamboat from Mobile to Point Clear, it had taken miracles to keep everything in good condition.

All her trunks now sat at the foot of her bed except for the trunk with her developing chemicals. Due to their toxic and flammable nature, she didn't want them with her. Plus, the management had insisted they be kept in one of the outbuildings until she needed them for her darkroom. Since most of her film wouldn't be developed until she returned home, she'd only need the darkroom for developing the photographs of the resort per the magazine's agreement with the owner. She'd photograph the management and staff, the guests enjoying the festivities at the resort, and schedule appointments with the guests for family portraits. Officially, she'd work three hours a day except on Sundays and had the freedom to take additional photographs at her leisure.

With her work not beginning until Monday, she could enjoy tonight's dinner and dancing plus the service in the morning. Surely, the resort provided a minister for the guests.

Amelia laced her shoes, wiping a smudge from the

brown leather toe of her left shoe, then stood from the bed and focused on her reflection in the mirror. She'd sent her black skirt to the laundry for cleaning after her collision with the boardwalk.

Tonight, her lilac chiffon dress with pink roses embroidered down the front had its chance to shine. The lace sleeves, which came to her elbows and boasted pink ribbons tied in bows, added an extra dose of gaiety to Amelia's heart. Aunt Patsy had insisted she bring the dress for dancing. Although she had no intention of dancing with anyone tonight or any night this summer, there was no harm in looking her best. Once guests found out she had come to take photographs of their families on holiday, they would expect someone who looked friendly, well-kempt, and professional all at the same time. So tonight, she'd make a favorable impression on as many as she could and hope her appointments filled up, leaving no gaps in her schedule.

A smile touched her lips as her eyes drew tight in a smile of their own. Would it be completely terrible if she danced tonight? Just one dance? She hadn't done so since the winter gala, and the only gentlemen who'd asked for her company on the dance floor were ones her aunts had pushed toward her. No one had awakened her heart, and since none had come calling, she must not have stirred any curiosity in them either.

Giving a twist to the left, then to the right, Amelia checked her reflection again. While she wasn't the most beautiful woman in the world, she had features men had complimented in the past. But to capture more than momentary attention from the gentlemen at the Grand, she needed more than a handsome appearance. She needed wealth and a desire to fill a home with children. She had neither. Mama and Pa hadn't left her with much when they passed, and her aunts weren't among Philadelphia's most elite. Given her chosen path of traveling for photography, she'd placed herself in an awkward position—one that very well could turn her into a spinster, as her aunts feared.

She shrugged.

No matter. None of that mattered this summer. Nor did it matter if she danced with any gentlemen tonight. She'd keep her expectations low because she'd most assuredly fail to meet the expectations of any of the gentlemen here at the Grand.

On her way out the door, she snatched her new Kodak Brownie camera. Perhaps if she found herself lacking in conversation, she could fill her time with capturing some of the evening's gaiety. And perhaps a stroll to the boardwalk could offer an opportunity to capture the sunset over the western horizon. A tingle jolted to her toes merely thinking about capturing a pelican in flight or a dolphin emerging from the sea. The evening held endless possibilities she could enjoy and whispered reminders of the promising days ahead.

ABOUT THE AUTHOR

Lisa M. Prysock is an award-winning, *USA Today* bestselling, Christian and inspirational author. She and her husband of more than twenty years reside in Kentucky. They have five children, grown.

She writes in the genres of both Historical Christian Romance and Contemporary Christian Romance, including a multi-author Western Christian Romance series, *Whispers in Wyoming*. She is also the author of a devotional. Lisa enjoys sharing her faith in Jesus through her writing.

Lisa has many interests, but a few of these include gardening, cooking, drawing, sewing, crochet, cross stitch, reading, swimming, biking, and walking. She loves dollhouses, cats, horses, butterflies, hats, boots, flip-flops, espadrilles, chocolate, coffee, tea, chocolate, the colors peach and purple, and everything old-fashioned.

She adopted the slogan of "The Old-Fashioned Everything Girl" because of her love for classic, traditional, and old-fashioned everything. When she isn't writing, she can sometimes be found teaching herself piano and violin but finds the process "a bit slow and painful."

Lisa enjoys working with the children and youth in her local church creating human videos, plays, or programs incorporating her love for inspirational dance. A few of her favorite authors include Jane Austen, Lucy Maude Montgomery, Louisa May Alcott, and Laura Ingalls Wilder. You'll find "food, fashion, fun, and faith" in her novels. Sometimes she includes her own illustrations.

She continues the joy and adventure of her writing journey as a member of ACFW (American Christian Fiction Writers) and LCW (Louisville Christian Writers). Lisa's books are clean and wholesome, inspirational, romantic, and family oriented. Discover more about this author at www.LisaPrysock.com where you'll find the links to purchase more of her books, free recipes, devotionals, author video interviews, book trailers, giveaways, blog posts, and much more, including an invitation to sign up for her free newsletter.

Links to Connect with Lisa:
https://www.bookbub.com/authors/lisa-m-prysock

Join Lisa Facebook Reader Group: https://www.facebook.com/groups/500592113747995/

https://www.goodreads.com/author/show/7324280.Lisa_M_Prysock

https://www.lisaprysock.com/sign_up_for_my_newsletter

ALSO BY LISA M. PRYSOCK

To Find a Duchess, Inspirational Regency Romance

The Christian Victorian Heritage Series
Hannah's Garden: a Turn of the Century Love Story
Abigail's Melody

The Lydia Collection
The Redemption of Lady Georgiana
Protecting Miss Jenna
Persecution & Providence

Arise Princess Warrior, a 30 Day Devotional Challenge

The Shoemaker, an Old-Fashioned Regency Christmas Story

Whispers in Wyoming
Dreams of Sweetwater River
Marry Me Katie
No Place Like Home
All That Glitters
The Legend of Lollipop
Holly for Christmas
Lost in Wyoming

Secret Admirer

Becoming Princess Olivia

<u>Brides of Grace Hill</u>

Geneva

Annabelle

Victoria

Tracy Jo, Coming Soon...

<u>Brides of Pelican Rapids</u> (Mail-Order Bride Series)

Lottie's True Love

Jenny's Secret Diary

Belle of the Ball

Josiah's Jewel

The Parson's Bride, A companion novel

Silver Aspen

The Prairie Princess

Hazel's Tribulations

<u>Holliday Island Resort</u>

Blitzen the CEO

<u>North and South</u>

Minnesota Bride

Silver Mountain

<u>Brides of Distinction</u>

A Valentine for Veronica

Find These Titles at

https://www.LisaPrysock.com

IF YOU ENJOYED THIS BOOK...

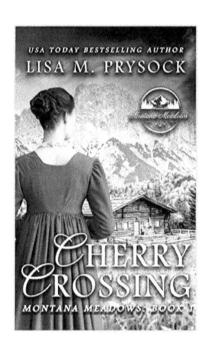

Cherry Crossing

If you love Christian Historical Westerns, check out this series about three sisters surviving in Montana during the 1870s.

Check out the book!

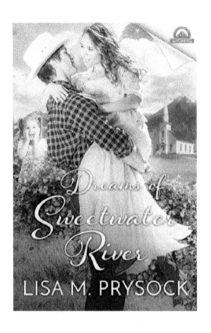

Dreams of Sweetwater River

Do you enjoy Christian Contemporary Western Romance? Check out this sweet, clean, and inspirational novel. Begin reading your copy today!

<u>Check out the book!</u>

If you love historical romance, check out the other Wild Heart books!

Marisol ~ Spanish Rose by Elva Cobb Martin

Escaping to the New World is her only option...Rescuing her will wrap the chains of the Inquisition around his neck.

Marisol Valentin flees Spain after murdering the nobleman who molested her. She ends up for sale on the indentured servants' block at Charles Town harbor —dirty, angry, and with child. Her hopes are shattered, but she must find a refuge for herself and the child she carries. Can this new land offer her the grace, love, and security she craves? Or must she escape again to her only living relative in Cartagena?

Captain Ethan Becket, once a Charles Town minister, now sails the seas as a privateer, grieving his deceased wife. But when he takes captive a ship full of indentured servants, he's intrigued by the woman whose manners seem much more refined than the average Spanish serving girl. Perfect to become governess for his young son. But when he sets out on a quest to find his captured sister, said to be in Cartagena, little does he expect his new Spanish governess to stow away on his ship with her six-month-old son. Yet her offer of help to free his sister is too tempting to pass up. And her beauty, both inside and out, is too attractive for his heart to protect itself against—until he learns she is a wanted murderess.

As their paths intertwine on a journey filled with danger, intrigue, and romance, only love and the grace of God can overcome the past and ignite a new beginning for Marisol and Ethan.

———

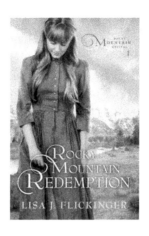

Rocky Mountain Redemption by Lisa J. Flickinger

A Rocky Mountain logging camp may be just the place to find herself.

To escape the devastation caused by the breaking of her wedding engagement, Isabelle Franklin joins her aunt in the Rocky Mountains to feed a camp of lumberjacks cutting on the slopes of Cougar Ridge. If only she could out run the lingering nightmares.

Charles Bailey, camp foreman and Stony Creek's itinerant pastor, develops a reputation to match his new nickname — Preach. However, an inner battle ensues when the details of his rough history threaten to overcome the beliefs of his young faith.

Amid the hazards of camp life, the unlikely friendship growing between the two surprises Isabelle. She's drawn to Preach's brute strength and gentle nature as he leads the ragtag crew toiling for Pollitt's Lumber. But when the ghosts from her past return to haunt her, the choices she will make change the course of her life forever—and that of the man she's come to love.

Lone Star Ranger by Renae Brumbaugh Green

Elizabeth Covington will get her man.

And she has just a week to prove her brother isn't the murderer Texas Ranger Rett Smith accuses him of being. She'll show the good-looking lawman he's wrong, even if it means setting out on a risky race across Texas to catch the real killer.

Rett doesn't want to convict an innocent man. But he can't let the Boston beauty sway his senses to set a guilty man free. When Elizabeth follows him on a dangerous trek, the Ranger vows to keep her safe. But who will protect him from the woman whose conviction and courage leave him doubting everything—even his heart?

CPSIA information can be obtained
at www.ICGtesting.com
Printed in the USA
JSHW050756140323
38916JS00008B/61